CW00471674

MERIDIAN

MERIDIAN:
A Day In The Life With Incidental Voices

by

David Rose

UNTHANK
BOOKS

First published in Great Britain in 2015
by Unthank Books of Norwich and London
www.unthankbooks.com

Text copyright © 2015 David Rose
Cover design © 2015 Sandy Cowell

The moral right of the author has been asserted

No part of this book may be used or reproduced in any
manner whatsoever without written permission from the publishers
except in the case of brief quotations embedded in critical
articles or reviews

Every reasonable effort has been made to trace copyright
holders of material in this book, but if any have been inadvertently
overlooked the publishers would be glad to hear from them

Unthank Books
PO Box 3506
Norwich
NR7 7QP

A CIP catalogue record for this book is available from
the British Library

ISBN 978 1 910061 05 3

Typeset in Garamond
Printed in China by KS Printing

For Caroline Clark
il miglior fabbro
&
Myriam Frey

What God in His curiosity needed was the *actuality* of the
world (*creatio ex ipse*).
St. Flavius
De Mundum I (iii)

The world is everything that is the case.
Wittgenstein
Tractatus I i.

$$Z \rightarrow Z^2 + C$$
Mandelbrot set

There will be resolution

Daybreak

*05.00 Pewter gleam of silver bevelled into focus, now with a dull green
sheen sweeping across from the luminous second- hand refracted by the bezel,
reflected by the handle of a glass carafe, now back to pewter, outlined against
a barely-perceptible undulant of quilted spread.*

*Wide-angle: a rectangle of low, chemically tinted light, a flickering band
of slightly stronger light slipping down the wall, dislocated by a bookcase,
randomly indented by the gaps in the spines, as the curtains belly in the night
breeze, parting at the join.*

(SAVE/<u>DELETE</u>)

*06.00 Chemical tinting now faded to natural daylight. Bedsheet and quilt
rucked back, terraced, now distinct in the dawn light.*

*Wide-angle: one curtain edge, vertically ruched, the other sheathed over
upper torso, male, the head invisible.*

(<u>SAVE</u>/DELETE)

I had opened the window to let in more air - I haven't been
sleeping solidly lately - stood leaning out for a while. It had been
raining in the night, sweetening the breeze. A shape, two shapes
emerged from beneath a parked car, clarifying into fox cubs,

playing tag and making a curious clucking noise which I realised was what had woken me. I looked at my watch. It was just after the hour, just too late for the camera, and in another hour they'll be gone. No matter; I've seen them.

The foxes, the fragrance, the first of the dawn choir – this too is valuable; this will be part of it.

07.00 Wedge shape, the two planes meeting in close-focus, one receding into shadow, the other striated by a bar of light reflecting from the polished wood, absorbed by the pit of the grain, the raw scuff on the angle edge, a broken splinter at 70 degrees, almost severed.

Wide-angle: marled colour field of dove grey, crossed by a path of light picking out a twist of white tissue, an irregular octagon of worn leather, a disc of discarded skin. Far left, an escarpment of rose pink, ridged, racked by cream tacking, beyond which a sequence of keys, slate grey, foreshortened. Flare of light from a falling cufflink.

(SAVE/<u>DELETE</u>)

08.00 Vertical column of matt rectangles in mottled ochre, raw umber, gamboge, raw sienna, with, lower left, approximate ellipse of sage green deepening toward the centre. Right column edge, a row of inverted U's, black paint layered, peeling back in patches, exposing weathered rust. Upper right, the railings obscured by felted leaves of soft viridian.

Wide-angle: footbridge pillar, railings interrupted by postered hoarding advertising cereal (Frusli), girl, red hair gathered behind, sitting on a backpack, man in houndstooth suit, pink buttonhole, carrying briefcase and cream plastic bucket. From platform end the rails streak away to converge behind ashes blued by the air.

(<u>SAVE</u>/DELETE)

I keep reading of the demise of the commuter, as more and more people work from home, log on in their kitchens, work in their pyjamas. It doesn't happen. Humans are gregarious, mostly. We need companionship, the reassuring interchange of trivia, the stimulation of chance encounters, fresh currents through our brackish selves. The irritation of delayed trains, subliminal tingling of the fear of crashes: even these are helpful in prodding our torpor, rendering tedium a welcome luxury.

It was musings like these that prompted me to embark on this. And the contradictory desires to live deeply in the present and to live beyond the present. The old dream of immortality in technological guise?

I don't think so. Closer maybe to leaving a butterfly collection to posterity. Or a sealed tomb for archaeologists. A desire for it all not to be wasted.

It seems on the face of it egotistical. But the ego is all we have. And a sufficient number of egos make a world.

The rain had long cleared up, leaving the last few clouds scrolling across the lower sky. You could smell the warmth, the scent of buddleia on the breeze.

The train, as it happens, was on time.

There were ticket inspectors at the barrier, on alighting; a jostle of people round the exit. The slow egress was caused by a girl – woman – without a ticket. Smartly dressed, business suit, laptop bag. Her season ticket, purse, money were missing. She was insisting she had a valid season ticket even though she couldn't produce it, suggesting, pleading, that they check the records. The inspectors, both of them, were adamant she produce it or be fined.

I bought her a single. The quickest way to disperse the jam.

She wanted to take my address, repay me; she explained that she had had an argument with her boyfriend the night before, over the unexpected result of a football match, which prompted him to throw her handbag through the window. She'd retrieved it in the dark, but her purse was still, presumably, in the rose bed.

Perhaps it was the sadness of her story that prompted what I later identified as paternal concern. If I had had a daughter, she would have been about the same age, with perhaps the same problems, same anxious desire to both please and be independent.

I refused her my address, telling her to pass on the good deed to someone else in the future, and we parted. But I thought of her all the way to my office.

09.00 Expanse of blue-gray slate, ocean-laid grain rippling under the polish, bounded at its far edges by stripped ebony. Immediate foreground, feather-rough blue of leather blotter. Middle ground, open rectangular frame, chrome and black lacquer, rows of globes of machine-polished steel holding taut the wire hawsers. Motionless.

Wide-angle: iron-grey carpet extended over the skirting and up the wall to approximately knee height, edged like the desk, with ebony, giving way to egg-blue emulsion. Left edge of vision, rhomboid of open door, polished cherry, sliver of corridor, herringbone parquet, polished.

(SAVE/DELETE)

I like to be at my desk well before nine, as an example to my staff, and to allow myself time to concentrate my mind.

As executive toys go, Newton's Cradles are now antique. No matter. The gentle clicking of the balls down to their point of rest, the voluptuous coolness of their polished surfaces drain the tensions, clear my mind.

Strange what effects physical surfaces have on our minds, our lives. In retrospect, I trace my decision to become an architect to the bricks I played with in early childhood.

They weren't wood but actual terracotta, matt glazed, a whole set in a wooden chest. They were passed on to me by an older cousin, whose father, my uncle, had bought them in Germany on a business trip, in the hope of encouraging more constructive tendencies in the character of my cousin, to no avail.

I loved them. Loved their shapes - cubes, oblongs, cylinders for columns, curved lintels - their texture, the smooth cool glaze on my cheek, though my attempts at actually building things were somewhat clumsy. Maybe poured concrete would have better suited my limited dexterity.

But, though I did later begin my architectural practice in the heyday of post-war modernism, when poured concrete was, so to speak, *de rigeur*, I retained a then nostalgic love of bricks, old and new, and their bonds and patterns, English Bond, Flemish Bond, Garden Wall, Running, Spanish, Basketweave ...

That did give me an advantage among traditionalist clients, while at the same time limiting my choice of commissions, and led to my specialising in modestly scaled dwellings – no landmark towers, prestige civil works, at least until brick made a comeback in the Eighties. But that was mostly Post-Modernist irony, and I've never been keen on irony in architecture. Buildings are not jokes; they have to stand up by themselves. Being true to one's materials doesn't allow bad faith.

This is also one of the reasons I've specialised in conversions. Working with what's already there brings limitations and limitation is the source of freedom. The instinctive response of any developer is to flatten the site, start from scratch. I try to dissuade them. A Tabula Rasa is another name for amnesia. There are cues from the architectural context, the neighbourhood, but they're too often ignored.

One of the buildings I'm most proud of came about that way. My client had acquired premises - the end of a row of Victorian shops (his had been a dairy). It was, admittedly, dilapidated, and his idea was, inevitably, to knock it down, replace it with the usual steel-glass-and-marble structure a storey higher.

I persuaded him to utilize the basement, punctuate the existing walls, and replace the roof with a dome of brick honeycombed with inset skylights and glass floor. Though modestly innovative, it fitted its environment, provided a smooth transition of axes on its corner site, and still had structural advantages – the strength of natural beehives, lightness, airiness. It won me a local architectural award and a small measure of notoriety at the time.

The idea for the roof had come to me over breakfast, looking at a jar of honey.

I went on, as a result of its success, to explore other organic structures over the years. My next was a cottage on a windswept coastal site, modelled on a snailshell – structurally one of the strongest forms in nature – of alternating spirals of dressed stone and glass brick.

Then an egg-shaped hangar in, this time, poured and polished concrete, the concrete dyed in the mixing to give a speckled finish. And not far from that, in the Lincolnshire fens, a hayrick-based house of reed-thatched walls of breezeblock and willow-and-thatch roof, with internal straw insulation against the raw East winds.

After that I went back – or forward – to re-exploring the rectilinear, the proverbial shoe-box. Actually, there is nothing aesthetically wrong with shoe boxes. And they are susceptible to interesting variations.

Such as my first – a low, single-storey dwelling with flat overhanging wrapped roof. The walls were unbroken except for a continuous strip of small windows at head-height running frieze-like round the whole building, the doors being glazed at the same height (including the internal doors). This was brick-red stretchers and blue headers.

It arose from a wager, a challenge from another architect to build an interesting shoe box. To prove my point, I bought a pair of Saxone brogues and copied the proportions of the box.

Sadly, despite its local award, it was later compulsorily purchased and demolished for a ring-road feeder. Until then, I'd become a frequent visitor, initially to sort out some problems with the concealed skylights, then as a guest of my client and his wife. Occasionally of his wife. It oscillated on the edge of an affair, then settled into a friendship, with both. After its purchase, some years later, they moved abroad and inevitably we lost touch.

I haven't thought of them in years. Suddenly, I miss them. Irretrievably.

10.00 Full field of vision an expanse of egg blue, matt at the peripheries, centrally shining, patterned with furrow from the drag of bristles.

Wide-angle: blue extending in both directions, broken in left field of vision by photograph – egg nestling in grass – partially obscured by reflection from glass; upper torso, female, tailored jacket, scarf wound and pinned below swept-up hair. Far left, slice of polished red wood.

(<u>SAVE</u>/DELETE)

It's surprising how dirty office walls become. Fingermarks, smudges, dents from rolled drawings. They affect my concentration. I've taken to keeping a tin of emulsion in the office cupboard, with a paintbrush and rubber gloves. I retouch the walls every so often. It's soothing. To the eye, the hand. The texture of the plaster.

The marks tend to congregate in the same places, related to the traffic flow. But occasionally one crops up in an out-of-the-way spot. I find myself conjecturing as to how they got there, reconstructing plausible scenarios for their random cause.

A swatted spider, perhaps. A flower thrown aloft in a fit of exuberance by my secretary. Perhaps not.

You can just see her in camera. Lovely girl. Linda. Couldn't manage now without her.

I first met her in a bar, which sounds as corny as you can get. Actually she was working there. I had taken a client for a drink, to finalise the window details of a conversion. She knocked over his glass of Peroni, over the plans, over his cuffs, his enamelled links dripping foam. He wasn't pleased and, to my embarrassment, made that abundantly clear. I went back to the bar after we parted, to apologise: I felt partly responsible. She was clearly upset – before the accident, I mean – grateful to talk.

Her boyfriend had committed suicide. He left no note; there had seemed no cause.

She looked at me I remember, her eyes bruised, almost frightened, by her bewilderment. 'He preferred death to me,' she said. 'Why?'

I wanted to put my arm round her, fold her into safety.

Instead, I offered her a job.

Have I succeeded in making her feel secure here? She's been with me some years, seems now to be happy, beginning to respond to flirtatious clients, casual dates, will one day risk commitment once more, and I will have to mentally let go, maybe even literally give her away – she has never mentioned her father, whether he's living or dead.

Has the pain been worth what I've given her? The pain to me, I mean. I sound her out gently after each date she mentions, wondering if this is the one for her.

But if she starts to go steady, I'll have succeeded. Won't I? There's consolation in that.

11.00 Jointed partitions forming apparently stacked wooden crates, but of ½» mahogany, varnished but chipped, matte in patches, bared wood splintered, darkened by the oblique fall of the light.

Wide-angle: boxes extend across to the left to edge of vision, partially to the right, then blank expanse of green-distempered plaster peeling back to mottled ochres. At extreme right, lightning flash of sky blue, flashes of bright red, fluorescent yellow, leaf green in descending view.

(<u>SAVE</u>/DELETE)

I was meeting a client here. He was a little late already. I don't mind lateness. Punctuality is for princes. If a man *does* something, he'll usually be late, sucked out of his schedule by the slipstream of events, contingencies. I like my clients to be late. It's a sign of success.

And I was glad of the chance to pause, stocktake, absorb the ambience of the project, take in the cues.

The problem for us all is that there is no dominant style now, no consensus-warp to cue us. International Style, Brutalism, PoMo - they're all *available*, which means *not defining*. We have to go it alone, select the cues.

This was once a Post Office. Purpose-built in standard Pre-War Civil Service: understated pediments, grey-blue stretcher bond, well-proportioned. An integrity I admire.

So, fortunately, does my client.

He found me by chance. He was driving through Norfolk, having been diverted by a flooded road, and came across my hangar. He traced its owner in the village, asked who the architect was, got in touch.

I like him. I like to get to know my clients, spend time with them, assess them as well as their needs, before agreeing to the project. He evidently does likewise. In the course of our first conversation, he suddenly pointed a finger-gun to my head, said 'What's the opposite of hibernation?' I thought for a moment, then replied 'Insomnia.' He said 'Okay, the job's yours.'

The steeply pitched roof has a large V in tiles distinct from the remainder. The story goes that the building was bombed during the war, though the bomb failed to explode. The two-finger sign was incorporated into the repair. My client told me that.

My surveyor told me the extent of the delayed damage, done not by the bomb but by an articulated lorry well after the war.

Demolition was an option – it's too damaged to be listed, even though it's the only building pre-dating the Sixties in this part of town. But there are other options, and ecological arguments for keeping 'found' buildings.

After it was decommissioned by the Post Office it became for a while a wine store. They kept the counter, and the sorting frames in the rear to store individual bottles. And the clock. But it's been empty for some years.

Even so, walking through it now I can still hear echoes of laughter from postmen long dead. That's the thing about old buildings, places of work. Work generates laughter, the jokey camaraderie of give and take. I can hear it swirl faintly from the high ceiling, leak from the pigeon holes of the sorting frames.

I've thought a lot about humour. Mainly because I've been told I don't have any. I've reflected on wit, jokes, puns. They intrigue me, satisfy me philosophically. Overlap of semantic plates, chance collisions releasing energy, sparks of light, warmth; worm holes in semantic space.

I thought about it again then – occasioned by the spectral laughter, but also by the crack down the wall. I went outside to look at it more closely. It jags down the whole height, from just below the roof. Over years of rain and wind it has acquired pockets of humus, now sprouts ferns in several places. There was one at chest height. I stopped to examine it. Beautiful in the sharp articulation of its fronds, greenly flaring against the stained brick. The fronds reminded me first of snow crystals, then of fractals, coral-clustering on the computer screen.

I went inside again. Daylight is clearly visible through the crack. It's irregular, but no doubt obeys laws of stress and impact. But its cause was random.

I laughed. It reminded me of an article I read some years ago in Architectural Review about a team of 'guerilla architects' given to using buildings as 'readymades' for subversive alteration. They were commissioned by a chain of merchandise showrooms – formula box-shaped brick supermarkets - to convert the buildings into public art.

The best-known, and BEST known (the name of the chain), in Virginia, involved knocking out a large rent in one wall, top to bottom, and allowing the outside vegetation to grow into the building.

I appreciate architectural wit as much as anyone, despite my reputation. I decided to do likewise. Keep the crack. Widen it maybe. The walls will need reinforcing anyway. I could utilise it, coat it in clear membrane, use it as a source of ventilation, natural daylight, a reminder of the vagaries of life outside.

I think the client will go with it. I can even see him commissioning a mural round it – Adam at the bottom left, a Godly finger top right.

Or again, we could plaster it with peat and plant it with moss, inside as well as out. As long as it's kept. I'd like, in fact, to incorporate it into a natural-draft cooling system. I still need to work out the airflow patterns for that anyway.

I walked backwards from the crack. With the shift in perspective, there was a flash of red. There's a pillar box outside, I remembered, and still in use – I heard the postman empty it just now.

The main facade and entrance also need strengthening. I could replace the portico and doors with a semicircular concrete drum to first floor height, automatic curved door, all in pillar box red. Single window grille above the door.

A PoMO pun perhaps. But I see it as more a response to contextual cues. And an elegant solution to practical problems. Structurally as well as stylistically functional.

I was keen to put these ideas to my client. It was already eleven thirty, and I was beginning to worry.

He didn't, in fact, show up at all. I hope he's alright. To lose the job would be a shame, but not a disaster. But I hope I haven't lost a potential friend.

Meridian

12.00 Right foreground broken by vertical bars of a wrought-iron gate of six foot height beyond which jets of water flower into plumes, blur of small bodies darting between. Across whole field of vision, distant railings to elbow height, glitter of water behind splinted trees.

Wide-angle: brick walls, windowed, at either side, at left paving slabs giving way to cobbles, recently laid. At extreme right the slanting plane of a stone plinth behind which stretch shadowed monumental wings.

(SAVE/<u>DELETE)</u>

With the non-appearance of my client I had time on my hands. I decided to walk back the long way, through the park, along the river.

I sat on one of the benches near the riverbank. On the next bench was a group of men of roughly the same age, probably alcoholics, certainly friends, not rowdy, not loud, simply conversing. I edged along my bench to listen. Maybe they noticed; I wasn't aware of it. But after a few minutes there was a change in tone.

- I met Bob yesterday mornin. Said he'd seen Jim Anson go by in a stretch limo.

- Stretch limo my arse. That was a hearse.

- Jim's dead? He didna tell me tha.

- He was winding you up. He's dead alright.

Their talk continued in reminiscence of the deceased. But it struck me that the exchange was so stagy it could have been rehearsed. I had become, perhaps unconsciously on their part, an audience, a chance to shine.

Is there a sociological counterpart to quantum mechanics? Even by eavesdropping, however discreetly, do we alter others' behaviour, even their memories?

I was struck again by how essentially unknowable, unreachable, we are to each other.

The group broke up after a while, leaving one of them alone amongst the empties. When the others had disappeared, he examined the bottles, shook the cans, gathered and put them carefully into a bin. He returned, not to his bench but to mine, eager, it seemed, for more conversation.

Now I was quite definitely an audience. Without need of enquiry he proceeded to tell me of his life, his wife, who had long since left, his squabbles with neighbours, victories over officialdom. My facing toward him was all the stimulus he needed. I merely listened.

After a while he invited me to join him in a drink. I wasn't keen, but noblesse oblige, and I did feel rather in need of one.

He stood up and walked carefully toward the railings on the embankment. I noticed what I at first took to be a tattoo on his back but which revealed itself to be a pattern of scars. His hair, though thinning, was shoulder length and surprisingly red in the sunlight, toning with the copper of his tan.

As he reached the railings a strange trick of light, caused, I now think, by the heat haze, made the air between us close behind him like a sliding door. I could just make out his shape as he knelt and tugged on a string.

He reappeared, shouldering through the density of air. He was cradling a dripping bottle of cider. He crouched and reached, pulling two plastic glasses from under his own bench, then sat down on mine.

I wiped my glass with a tissue as discreetly as I could, pretending to blow my nose, and held it out to the bottle as he poured. The cider was river-cooled, surprisingly good.

But he pulled a smaller bottle from the shirt at his feet, said 'Splash of vodka in that? Can't drink it neat,' emptied a third into my glass before I could remove it.

Alcohol works quicker if you sip it slowly. I swallowed mine down. It made no difference.

I tried to concentrate on remembering the density of air, aware of him talking, something to do with the Benefits Agency. To the right of the bench the council have installed a water feature for children, sending six foot jets into the air whenever someone approaches. Someone had, and the light flashed and danced across the newly-relaid expanse of turf between fountain and benches. I heard him say *grassed up* and I said, Yes, they've done a good job, the public should be grateful.

I'm not sure why but he took sudden violent umbrage at my remark, swore effusively and snatched back the glass. I attempted an apology but by now he had sunk back into himself, into a remote zone of unreachable distrust. I got up and left him.

I looked back to the bench from the gravel path. He was already swallowed from my view by the shimmering heat.

Air pressure at sea level is 15lb. per square inch.

a

I'll go to the offy in a mo, get some reinforcements. It's going to be a warm one this afternoon. These benches should be awned, or moved to the shade.

- They're bolted down.

- Bloody typical, council. All that council tax, they worry about a few benches going missing, sod the taxpayer.

- You don't pay council tax.

- Course I fuckn pay it.

- Your is paid by the government.

- Deducted out of my money, though. Course I fuckn pay it. Might be deducting even more soon. Someone's shopped me to the Bennies.

- Who was tha?

- How should I know? Some nosy bleeder. Must've seen me doing that wall at 73, as a favour, like. Only repairing it to where those fuckn kids had pushed it over. Not like doing a whole wall from scratch, is it? They're coming to interview me Tuesday. Early I hope.

- Tuesday Foxy comes out.

- Seen him, then?

- Wouldn't let me in.

- Shouldn't be sleeping rough at his age.

- He doesna have to. He's got a gaff.

- Either way, no excuse for beating him up. What'd they expect to get out of him?

- You takes your choice, you takes your risk. Why sleep rough if he doesna have to?

- Likes the fresh air.

- Did I tell you this? I was talking to Jerry last week, says a mate of his knows of a bloke, younger than Foxy, living rough, dossing around, somebody bought him a flat.

- Flat what?

- A flat, a dwelling, an apartment, what d'you think?

- Just like tha?

- More or less. Touched him for a drink like, bloke starts asking him questions, how come he's homeless, how long, and so on, so he tells him the story. Bloke takes him to an estate agent, buys him a flat. On condition he sorts himself out, cleans himself up. Only a *small* flat, course.

- Come on.

- True as I'm sitting here. Jerry says his mate swore to it.

- In the City, was this?

- Didn't say. Only that the bloke's rich, obviously, homes all over the world, appreciates his luck.

- Hedge fund?

- It's a flat. No garden, is there?

- Christ, why couldn't we meet someone like that?

- Because we're not dossing, are we?

- So did he?

- Did he what?

- Sort himself out, clean up his life?

- Gather so.

- It's no so easy, flat or not.

- T managed it, no help from no one. Will power. Put his life back on the even. Reckons he's setting up a charity. Vagrancy outreach. Wouldn't put it past him, neither.

- Yeah, but he's still young.

- Too late, even so. Wife, pretty woman too, nice home, kids - she's remarried now.

- So could T if he wants. Young enough.

- Jim Anson did, remember? Older than T. Doing well for himself now.

- I met Bob yesterday mornin. Said he'd seen Jim Anson go by in a stretch limo.

- Stretch limo my arse. That was a hearse.

- Jim's dead then? He didna tell me tha.

- He was winding you up. He's dead alright.
- But he was doing so well. On the wagon.
- There's other things apart from booze kills you.
- I keep telling my doctor tha.
- What killed Jim then?
- There's different theories. Don't let this spill out. You know he married that woman, widow, with the ice cream business. Some say he was servicing the van, had it jacked up, like, jack slipped. But there's word out he was cut up. Wasn't just serving vanilla cones from that van.
- He was dealing?
- No way. Jim?
- Think he got those flash clothes from ice cream?
- You can make a fair pile in season.
- What about out of season?
- Told me he was out most of the year.
- Exactly. Who'd buy ice cream in the cold?
- Kids.
- It was the college he'd park himself by, not the infants.
- This really on the level?
- That's the word.
- Christ. He'd ha lived longer staying drunk.
- Pity he ever met the merry widow.
- She didn't come from the estate, though. Respectable road. Semi-detached, curtains.
- When it comes down to brass tacks, most respectable people are fuckn bent.

b

On you go to the Alpine House then, I'll stay here among the grasses.

Bent, fescue, meadow foxtail. Even the names are feathery, aren't they? Not the Latin. Those are as severe as the square neat beds. When you've gone and there's no one watching I'm going to take a few seed heads, hide them in my map, and plant them in the garden, release them from their boxed beds, let them spread and run wild, as they should, as they would in the wild, in the prairies, rolling for miles, inland oceans, that's what I'll think of, if they grow. I'll dig up the lawn, you can help me, do the digging, get rid of the sedate suburban lawn, Alfred Lawn Tennyson, that's from Joyce, isn't it? You would know. Plant real grass instead. Start a Campaign For Real Grass. That's apt, too, isn't it? Campaign is from *field*, only for us it conjures death fields, battle fields, but if we were French we'd think of picnics, drinking champagne and eating *champignons*, those wild mushrooms you like in risottos.

The only drawback is you can't sit on real grass, just walk through it, feel it, mow it twice a year. Have to use a scythe, I should think, that would be part of the campaign, real tools, hand tools, like those you bought me.

The coast is clear now. *Agrostis tenuis*, Common Bent, an ear of that. *Bromus mollis*, Soft-brome. Red Fescue, *Festuca rubra*. You really wouldn't approve of this, would you? *Anthoxanthum odoratum*, Sweet Vernal grass. See what I mean about the Latin? Crested Dog's Tail. Quaking grass. *Holcus lanatus*, Yorkshire-fog, must have some of that.

We never got to the Dales, did we? You dragged me round the industrial museums for three days and by then the weather had changed.

Why did we never go back?

You were full of it on the way home, talking of Bessemer converters and crucible steel. I mentioned Blake's dark Satanic mills, and you explained - at length - that he was talking of the mechanistic Newtonian universe, not factories, that Blake was a Gnostic.

You began making miniature steam engines in the spare room. I thought I was losing you, becoming a model widow, you were always in there. And maybe it was my fault, in a way. That L. S. Lowry print I bought you, that perhaps was the spark.

I always thought it odd, though. You later took it off the living room wall, hung it in the spare room, your model room. And soon after that you hardly went in there.

I never liked to ask why. I was pleased to have you back, have some help in the garden. I wondered, though. Had a model blown up? I couldn't see any scalding. But you were withdrawn, after that. I'd lost you even more, and you never really came back. You became quite keen on gardening, planting on your own initiative, vegetables, bulbs, later Alpines. But there was part of you missing, a sort of optimism.

You stopped winding the hall clock. You'd always taken pride in its accuracy, adjusting the weights every week. Then you muttered something about the escape. You bought a battery powered quartz clock instead. You never explained.

Tufted Hair grass, an ear of that. This map's bulging. I'll wrap these in my handkerchief. Do you remember the antique reed trug you gave me for my birthday? Somewhat battered, but still beautifully light and balanced. Then, I think, the following Christmas, those even older snippers. You said they were for me, but you spent the holiday oiling and grinding them, then used them yourself in the summer, dead-heading the roses.

I wondered if collecting antique gardening tools would become your next passion, but somehow there hasn't been another passion. Not even your gardening.

Some of the trainees are weeding, working toward us. One more while they're not looking. *Poa pratensis*, Smooth Meadow-grass. Green and pleasant.

Do you remember the time we were listening to the Last Night of the Proms on the wireless, and they began the customary outing of 'Jerusalem' and you said 'cant' and switched it off?

c

Must, say the experts, should be between 19° and 24° C. before adding the yeast, so he puts the bucket back on its stand above the boiler, thoroughly wipes the thermometer and puts it in its box, then attends to the racks. Wine for laying down should ideally be stored at a cant of 10° rather than absolutely flat, to avoid corking, so he has measured, mitred, cut and planed four wedges, a pair for each rack, then varnished them for durability. He has now simply to drill the bottom struts of the racks, countersink the holes, and screw the brass screws through into the corresponding holes in the wedges, and that's another job done, by which time the must might be ready.

He takes off his tie prior to the exertion.

Maybe he shouldn't have worn a tie on the programme. Maybe that would have helped, a little at least. He had intended to wear a bow tie, the silk one he kept for special occasions, and appearing on television was as special an occasion as he would experience now in his life. But the wardrobe lady had dissuaded him. It was all about 'image' these days, he understood that. She had suggested an open-neck shirt, but he felt, he knew, the 'image' would have miscued. A tie and fully buttoned shirt helped hide the wattled neck men of his age displayed. No, he had held firm on the tie, choosing one that complemented his counter-pane check jacket and viyella shirt. She had raised the idea of a cravat, but that was well beyond the pale these days, unless one lived in Windsor. No, no, he was confident in his judgment.

But it would have made no difference as it happened. He might as well have worn a spotted, revolving bow-tie, he'd have appeared no more foolish.

He has put one rack on the draining board, lined up the wedge, dropped in a screw, but it's tricky getting the screwdriver at the right angle because of the size of the gap between the struts of the rack. He's allowed for the angle in drilling the wedges but the screwhead simply isn't going to fit flush into the countersinking, so there's going to be the danger, however small, of catching his finger on the screw's edge when lifting out the bottom bottles, if he held them by the neck, at any rate. He doesn't want to file down the screwhead, it would look rough, bodged.

He drops in the first screw of the other wedge, finger-tightens it to hold the rack even, then finishes tightening both screws on the first wedge. It had all come down to one letter. If there'd been no R in the random letters.

He drops in the second screw of the second wedge, tightens them both as hard as he can, runs his finger gingerly over the proud side of the screwheads.

Then he would simply have plumped for *cottage*. His opponent, cocky little bloke, probably a teacher, had had *courtage* - was there such a word? They'd checked in Dictionary Corner and said there was. Without the R maybe he too would have gone for *cottage*, or maybe found another eight-letter word, and won. That wouldn't have mattered. He didn't mind losing – he'd lost anyway in the tie-breaker anagram, flustered by the audience reaction when he'd announced his word, and the fleeting look of amused horror on Des' face. It had made him uncomfortable, for he hadn't understood.

At least his opponent had shaken hands gracefully, although he'd earlier been concealing what could be described as a smirk.

He'd thought about it all the way home in the train, to no avail. Not until he'd gone to the Reference Library and looked it up in the complete Oxford.

He wasn't a prude, not in the least. Good God, worse things than that had happened during the war. It was just, the discomfort, the discomfort of feeling at last out of date. He'd prided himself on keeping abreast. He had Broadband, ordered things on it, like the wine racks, not groceries though, he enjoys the stroll and the company of queuing. He even helps some of the others in the club with the Internet.

But he remembers now being in a Post Office queue once. The woman in front was putting money into savings accounts for her sons, who were evidently grown up by then. Yes, she saying to the clerk, I've been putting money aside for them since they were little. Oh yes, both my sons are well-endowed.

He remembers discreetly joining in the laughter, which wasn't malicious, not at all, in fact there'd been, on his part at least, a tinge of compassion at the woman's faux pas, at which she herself had been blissfully unaware. It was in fact pity he had felt as she walked away, and pity above all is what he most dreads.

The programmes were pre-recorded, he understood that. Maybe then they would decide not to screen it.

They'll all be watching at the club of course. He'd told them all, at least he'd told Hilda Unsworth, which was much the same thing. They'd think he'd been stringing them along. No matter. Better that way.

Then again, if they were to screen it, there'd possibly be no one in the club who'd know the word anyway. But no, someone was bound to. And they'd still notice his reaction. Best keep his head down, skip the club for a while.

No, the real quandary is Valerie. How to play it.

He lifts the rack down to the floor, testing for any wobble. Pleasingly sturdy. He lifts the other rack onto the draining board, sides up the wedge. Should he play up his man-of-the-world approach, pretend a daring mock-innocence on the show? The angle of the screwhole is not right, he's having to force it, hoping the slot doesn't burr. She might, though, get the wrong idea. Good God, just when she's beginning to open up.

The screwhead's held. Play it by ear, then. She certainly wouldn't know the usage, even as a crossword addict. Maybe she'd respect more his old-fashioned innocence. The last screw threads in sweetly. But his appeal to her is precisely that he's not old-fashioned. Not like some in the club. She'd told him that.

He lifts the rack to the floor, flexes it gently, carries both racks to their allotted place under the stairs.

They're a good fit there, pleasing. But somehow a bit silly, being empty. And there's the dust.

He knows in his work chalet he has some deal boards. Cut them to size, neat tongue-and-groove, French polish.

d

Words are not needed in putting in a bid so her stutter doesn't matter, just a nod or a wave, even raised eyebrows will secure it, so she feels she's dancing now, the muttering in her ear urging her on as one by one the bidders drop out, and though she's nearing her limit he's still whispering her on, raising the ceiling, insistent on the deal, until the tilt of her head is followed by a pause then the gavel hits home.

Still no speech required, just her signature and a smile. Mr. Avramati is whispering his pleasure. There's a break in the sale now, a general stir. The heat draws the dust from old upholstery. She closes her eyes. This is what she is paid for, this recreative vision.

She pushes through the crowd to examine again, for pleasure, her pleasure, the lot she has secured. Staffordshire spaniels, a pair, seated, flower baskets in mouths, chip to the rear on one, noted; runs her fingers over the cool glazed backs and is back in her grandmother's, quiet and safe, stutter momentarily gone, forgotten. They, basketless, slightly taller, haughtier, flanked the fireplace. They too were cool, even in the coal-glow. She could sense their response beneath the china disdain. She never spoke, never talked, not to them anymore. She had a friend for that.

Above them on the mantelpiece a softly tocking bracket clock, fluted creamware candlestick, chipped and empty, oval ivory pot and lid, grainy like fingernails. Beyond the firepool and island rug, across the polished linoleum, the glass-fronted cabinet, thought to be Regency, with its exquisite odour as you opened the door. This cabinet – she has already described it minutely to Mr. Avramati, including the rosewood-and-polish scent – she has still in her sight as she travels the markets, scours the catalogues.

She has had it in her grasp several times but each time let it go. A hint of woodworm, a broken hinge … Mr. Avramati, and her childhood, deserve perfection.

Its contents she has already assembled: Victorian castletop vinaigrette; dragon-handled cloisonné bowl; Worcester sauce-boat, lettuce leaf-shaped with painted insects; Derby shepherdess.

The intermission is over, she moves back to her place, fanning gently with her catalogue. She has starred, and examined, two more lots: a pair of copper deep-bottomed pans, and six Victorian wired-stoppered pickle jars.

Jam, for her, means freedom, expansion of her soul. The clatter of copper pans in her grandmother's kitchen was the comfort-zone of solitude, of being left alone to *be*, to converse with her friend unpressured until called into the kitchen to taste the jam as it cooled like lava on the biscuit.

All that was required of her was her opinion of the jam, in measurable terms - more sugar or less, damson or plum - with time to taste and answer.

Then she and her grandmother would sit and rest on the rush-seated chairs (she's still searching for these) enjoying the quiet metered out by the pendulum (that clock she has long-since secured) until time for home, friend in her head.

Now Mr. Avramati is her invisible friend. She autodials him to reassure him of the provenance of the pans, the authenticity of the denting, for «'authentic' is the watchword», nothing vulgar, nothing *faux*, nothing to dispel the *echt*-English haphazardness.

She has made her unpressured assessment, a simple yes-no. She need express no opinion with Mr. Avramati beyond that decision. No agonies of degrees, of calibrated choices, of co-option by competing sides, by parents she loved equally, pushed into the refuge of that prevaricating stutter.

She can relax now, his whisper in her ear, to the cut of the bidding. The dilettantes are dropping out, it's resolving again into the game she enjoys, a badminton against one rival, a binary series of lobs. She is determined to win; Mr. Avramati is willing her on.

And, she has yet to tell him, she has spotted a Beswick «cottage» cheese dish in a little shoppe on the way, to complement the teapot, sugar bowl and milk jug. This is proving a rewarding day. Mr. Avramati will deem it a Red Letter day. Which always saddens her. For one thing from her childhood she has not described or mentioned, being for her too personal even for imaginary friends: a needlework sampler, a calendar of the year it was stitched, showing in red the Ember Days of that year.

She would think, every time she saw it, of a Sunday School scripture, the seraphim taking with tongs an ember from the altar, touching it to the lips of Isaiah, to cleanse, salve, permit him to speak the Lord's words with no hesitation, impediment.

Despite her discovery that the dates were merely the feast days of the four seasons, three for each, Lent, Whitsun, September and December, no connection at all with glowing coals, she still thinks of Red Letter days as days of healing. She feels a slight disloyalty for leaving out the sampler in her inventory of childhood. So now she concentrates – 35 40 45 46 – so tonight she can enjoy in silence the larval flow of Mr. Avramati's praise – 47 *no advance on 47?* ...

e

As long as it's still there, although in a way he hopes it isn't because if it is still there this late in the year it would obviously be injured, a wing most likely, but if it is still there, if it isn't a wind-up, God let it not be a wind-up, he will have seen it, some good will come out of it, even its injury, which he hopes is healing, the wing or whatever, so it can catch next season's migration north.

He's checked the guide books. There *have* been Great Northern Divers this far inland, in winter of course; they've been recorded on these Wraysbury lakes – really gravel pits, a chain, disused and reverted to scrub – and on the reservoirs in nearby Windsor. And the phone base, though amateur, is usually reliable.

So he sits in the train out with two pairs of bins (one long-range), monopod, thermos and waders, pulling out of Ashford – he wonders if people ever get out here expecting the Eurostar station, wonders if his trip will be equally disappointing – with two stops to go.

He polishes the lenses of the short-range bins, the 10x42's, Opticrons, he'd taken out a loan to buy them, cheaper that way than hire purchase and long-since paid off. He thinks of his first pair, Russian-made. second-hand. Bought, in fact, to help a mate, flogging off his stuff to raise the fare to the States. Bought purely as a favour. They came in an old-fashioned plush-lined case of real leather. And the lenses, his mate said, were Zeiss. Because after the war, the Russians dismantled factories wholesale, moved them lock, stock and barrel back to Russia as enforced reparation.

That information alone was worth the asking price. Being born too late to remember much of it, he had read up on the war. As a boy he'd read the War Picture Library comics, hidden from his parents. Later had read serious histories of the conflict, the build-up, the battles. But they all ended at VE Day.

So all this was new to him, the returnees, the expulsions, the Displaced Persons housed in barracks, prisons, derelict halls, or left to wander, fend off reprisals, drinking from gutters, gleaning the fields. The looting, the proud abjection. The Montan-Union. A whole new field. Life, he found, was a constant rippling out.

But he'd still had no use for the binoculars. No good for the stars. Dangerous to spy on neighbours. So he'd taken up bird-watching. A whole new world. A new, wholly non-human, world. It pleased him.

He started by taking his binoculars to work, kept them in the cab of his float. On days off, before he retired, he would get up the same time, walk over the common. Or take the train to Barnes to the Wetland Centre, where he fell in love with the wildfowl. Their size, colouring, the fact that they were easier to spot than warblers in trees. But something more; the combination of birds and water ...

He had watched Smew, Goosander, Pochard, Grebe. But no Divers. It was Divers he found most fascinating in the books.

Partly it was a joke, a phrase, a bubble nudged from the silt of memory. *Don't forget the diver.* He couldn't quite place it. An advert, maybe. But apart from such subliminal ripples, he found them such utterly beautiful birds. Their markings, silhouette, their trailing links with the remote North.

Red-throated, Black-throated. Great Northern (glamour of steam that name conjured up). Like film stars, he knew them only from photos.

Two summers ago, a Great Northern was reported to be breeding in Scotland. He had flown north.

It had proved a wild goose chase. Literally. The Ember Goose, Immer Goose, *Gavier immer*, never appeared. A misattribution, mistaken identity?

It had still been worth the trip – he had headed south west, to the shores of Loch Frae, hired a scope, waited his turn in the hide for a glimpse of *Gavia stellata*. the Red-throated diver, on its nest of moss, its throat patch dulled in the misty light but nevertheless …

He's not a twitcher, lister, completist at all. He knows there are birds he will never see. The White-billed Diver, the Spoonbill, Little Bittern … But his sights are still set on the Great Northern Diver. So he's hoping today for an ironic twist of nature, to glimpse one on his doorstep in gravel pits near Staines.

He alights at Wraysbury, an unmanned station, quiet between the commuter hours. He steps out of the station straight into the complex, a series of lakes surrounded by willows, elder, nettles. There's a wide expanse of grass and scrub dotted with burnt-out cars. In the distance he can see two more, not yet junks, being raced by kids in a cloud of gravel dust. He turns away, follows the bank of the first of the pits.

There's not much on the water – mallards, of course, Tufted ducks, a Great Crested Grebe. He works methodically around the pit, walks to the next, bigger, irregular. He swings off his backpack, takes out the high-powered bins, 20x60's, screws them to the monopod, slowly quarters the open water. A Little Grebe emerges from the reeds, followed by several juveniles. Further off, the bottle green head and spade-like bill of a Shoveler. No Diver.

There's a bay beyond, obscured by willows. Rather than make the detour he decides to move into the water. Takes off his shoes. It's too hot for waders, he rolls up his trousers instead, peels off his socks, steps cautiously out. It will shelve steeply and suddenly, so he takes his time, feeling his way with his bare feet as he moves the monopod, scans *forget* the water. Mud like velvet.

It's deepening *don't forget* now, dropping away. He steps back a pace. Still *diver* no sign. Bubbles float up, a submerged pocket dislodged in his mind.

A game. Four, five of them. In the swimming pool, school visits. One held down under the water as the others chanted. Don't forget the diver. Always he was the one held down. Always. The others, holding him, would also be submerged, but they changed over, held him in relay.

He had had to work out a survival method. Fill his lungs before (knowing it would come), let out the air slowly in bursts, then hold it. Once they saw no more bubbles, they would panic, let go.

In the holidays, they would go to Langham's Pond. Muddy, no chlorine of course, the silt like silk. He longed always to burrow his fingers into it, but couldn't risk dislodging bubbles. They grew impressed with his prowess at staying under, never sure how long to hold him, how far to gamble. But the more confident he got, the less fun for them.

Then one boy brought his little sister. One, maybe two years younger. They sat on the bank, handing round Tizer, aniseed balls. Then one shouted, Don't forget the diver, another shouted, Susie. They dragged her in, held her down.

She struggled. He knew she would be unprepared. He waded in, his delight in the victim being someone else now overtaken by worry, pushed them away. They let her up. Suddenly, maybe, felt cheated. As she scrambled onto the bank, two of them pulled off her knickers, threw them into the nettles.

One of them was him.

They stood in a circle as she cried, shivered in the middle.

After what was probably no more than a minute, her brother darted into the nettles, plucked out her sopping knickers, threw them to her. Went in search of dock leaves.

He fished Langham's Pond. Years later. For tench. Nosing their way across the silt, nudging the reeds. When he had fished enough, he would wade barefoot, occasionally, when hot, submerge himself.

He has forgotten all this. Likewise forgotten, almost, Julie. Twelve years later, maybe thirteen. Their last encounter, their first and last attempt at sex. On his spread mackintosh in a thicket of hawthorn. Velvet texture of her skin under his fingers. Then, as she quickened, the silken tench-like slime as he eased down her knickers. In her excitement, she cried and flailed. He panicked, shrank.

She had stalked off, swearing.

He replayed it, over and over, varying the outcome, the possibilities. Always in subaqueous silence.

In time, the silt resettled.

He treads carefully back to the bank, clips the covers over the lenses, lays down the monopod, pours some iced tea. The stock cars have gone. In the heat, below the unheard rumble of aircraft, it's quiet, as quiet as his flat. Still, he's pleased the Diver has gone, if indeed it was ever here, away from the din and junk, back to the cold, clear, silent waters of the north.

The monopod between his legs, he sweeps the bins across the scrub, back to the cliff-like gravel bank. There are sand martins, he can see the network of holes, the martins over the water.

He swings higher, catches something hovering, a kestrel, high up. It drops, hovers again.

It's not a kestrel, tail's too short. He stands, extends the monopod, refocuses. He can make out the black moustache on white collar, the chestnut thighs. It's a Hobby.

He's entranced. They're rare, he's never seen one before. Entranced, yet uncertain, uncertain of his feelings. That old, familiar mixture of elation and disgust. He shares the usual fascination with birds of prey, the acrobatic marvels, the prowess, power. But.

The Hobby climbs, swerves, suddenly stoops, diving down, a martin darting, twisting, but unmatched to the hobby's speed it's taken, in one fell swoop.

He collapses the monopod, unscrews the binoculars, trying to place the quotation, Shakespeare, yes, but which?

Whatever his feelings, it's a first for his log.

As he walks to the station, it comes to him. The diver. A radio show. Tommy Hanley. ITMA.

f

- There. That's the last placard.

- 'FELL/ATIO SUCKS'. I don't see the connection with an anti-fur protest.

- It's a pun. 'Fell' is Old English for a skin, a pelt. From the Old Frisian.

- Little arcane, isn't it?

- That's the idea. Make them think. Not that they will. Or can. But even fashionistas have dictionaries, some of them. Besides, there's the B-side.

- 'How Do You Like Your Hide Tanned?' Lacks the subtlety of the A-side, perhaps. Still very   direct, sexually oriented.

- Sex is what it's all about. You think fur coats are about keeping warm?

- I still think the anti-fur message is rather hidden.

- O.k., there's a third.

- 'Full Pelt To Extinction.' More to the point. But is this the right time of year for an anti-fur protest?

- Now is when they buy them, to put into cold storage. Besides, fur's cropping up in all the new season's collections. Galenzi's showing fur collars and cuffs for spring. Jo Prinz is showing muffs and Alice bands.

- Hence the placard over there? 'Keep Cats Off The Catwalk.' As in Naomi Campbell?

- As in feline fur. That one's literal. Did you know there are places in Europe that advertise as cat sanctuaries so they can sell their skins? We're talking Western, not Eastern, here. As in Switzerland, to be exact.

- I'd have to substantiate that.

- You're too late. It's already been in the press.

- It doesn't matter. I'm more interested in doing this as a rounded piece, sort of personal profile of a typical protester.

- There *is* no typical protester.

- Sorry. Alright, one in particular. But I hope, fairly representative.

- I represent only myself. And the cause.

- The Fur Brigade. Tell me, what do you do in the close season? Between the collections and the time women actually wear them?

- Oh, there are plenty of other things, sadly. Horse racing. We're planning to disrupt next year's Grand National, for example.

- Why?

- Do you know how many horses are put down every year in steeplechasing?

- How many?

- I shan't tell you. You'll only want it substantiated. Find out for yourself. But if the jockeys were put down as well, the figures would drop.

- So you're planning to throw yourself under the horses at Aintree? Hasn't that already been done? Emily Davison?

- That was Ascot. In 1913. And for the vote.

- You think the vote for women wasn't important?

- What have we done with it? But you're right, the suffragettes set a precedent. Letter bombs, arson attacks on politicians' estates, trains and phone lines sabotaged. People have forgotten that. Personally, I may emulate Mary Richardson.

- ?

- She slashed a Velasquez in the National Gallery. I'd choose a Munnings. Or a Stubbs.

- I assume you're a vegetarian?

- Of course I'm a bloody vegetarian.

- Isn't that an oxymoron?

- Precisely. And talking of morons... Actually, that was the start of it, for me. Meat. Lamb. A leg of lamb. I was thirteen or so. We had a roast every Sunday. And chops, steaks, through the week. But that week's joint was – leg-shaped. On the dining table, waiting to be carved, you could see what it had been. I could see the lamb, in a field. I'd always had pets - rabbits, hamsters, a chinchilla, and we'd always had meat. But you just don't connect them. I did with that joint. I tried to eat it. It choked me, literally. I said it was a bit of bone. But after that… Eventually my mother accepted it, just served me the vegetables. The others teased me. Miss Tapioca, my father called me. But. I knew I was right.

- But from meat to slashing Stubbses?
- Logic. You have to accept the logic.
- But if the logic leads you to finally unethical actions?
- Then the initial premise is wrong. This one's right.
- Logically, then, you're a vegan?
- Of course.
- Are there any male vegans? All those I've met have been female. 'Women are from Vegas …'
- Witty! I know some.
- But surely now, ecologically, plastic alternatives to leather pose ethical problems? Logically.
- My shoes are jute.
- A new invasion?
- Why are journos so fucking flippant?
- Gives us buoyancy, against the flood of opinions. Can we backtrack a little? What was your turning point from passive vegetarianism to full-blooded animal rights?
- It was hardly full-blooded, to begin with. Milk-and-water, actually. Literally. At about fifteen I decided to proselytize, so to speak. Mount a protest at a nearby farm. It happened to be a dairy farm. I didn't understand the difference. Made my first boyfriend through it. Same school, a year ahead. He offered to help me with the placards - he was good at carpentry. Then we paraded up and down along the fence. It was only a public footpath, and very few public. Then the cows suddenly charged, several of the posts looked rather loose, we decided to hang the placards on the fence and retreat.
- And the boyfriend?
- It turned out – predictably – it was *my* udders he was interested

in. Lasted no longer than the protest.

- What about these placards? If the cows charge? If it gets rough?

- I've toughened up since then. We have a few tactical manoeuvres in mind, some pre-emptive hardware: paintball guns, stink bombs, pepper. If the police are there, we're okay. If they've hired private muscle, we're buggered. But it's on par, it's the price. A small enough price. The animals were buggered with an electric gad.

g

Are any of you old enough to remember *Sydney Greenstreet?* '*By Gad, sir, you're a character, that you are...*' *Maltese Falcon, must've seen it. Humphrey Bogart, Peter Lorre. Know the best thing about Lorre? His articulation.* Fuck, where is this going? Film noir, film noir... *Film noir. I watch a lot of films noir. My television's still black and white.* No, make that *an old black and white.* No, that's a tautology these days. *Still monochrome?* Too technical, not punchy. God, where's this going, going nowhere, new tack. God, Gad, gadzooks, begad. *Begad* is from *bigot.* Bigotry? No. Every fucking comedian in the country's doing bigotry. Become obligatory.

A pro-bigotry bash? Anti-anti-bigotry rant? Not many sacred cows left to milk. Find something. Greenstreet. Obesity? Fattism. *Greenstreet. More of a boulevard. Danna ... danna ... danna ... danna FAT MAN. Holy Smoke. Fat Man meets the Thin Man. Puff. Matter and anti-matter. Cancel each ... Black Hole* sucked into one now teacher once, what was his name, all called him Burp, triple chin, looked like he was just about to Geography he took poster back of the classroom double globe Atlantic Americas one Pacific Australia on the I drew legs on both glasses eyebrows first one fringe of his hair just below China the other never knew whether he twigged started calling him Charles Atlas 7 ton weakling couldn't control couldn't go to the Bod either without admitting grudge match for me sarcastic old sod. Gilbert Jewish boy Burp started making feeble kipper jokes Yom Kippur war was on Gilbert not even kosher made no difference. So. I started doing sardine jokes. Crossed out ITALY on the map altered it to GREATER SARDINIA. Took in a D. H. Lawrence book 'Sea And Sardinia' read it in his class. Every question on Natural Resources all answered 'sardines'. Tins of them in his briefcase. Then tins in his desk drawer. Opened.

Went on to whales pinned up posters Hump-backs started

calling him Humpy   left next term early retirement often wondered still 'sticks and stones' sorry for him in a way all of us blinkered only way to see ahead where'd I? Scrap Fat Man. Bogart Bogey Colonel? Guinness *Remember Alec Guinness? Had a head on him. Great actor. Bridge On the River Kwai. Making a sequel. Backgammon In Burma* no *On the Ganges* back to sacred cows Hindu Kushty this is crap, and only, Christ, half a minute's worth of crap.

h

until they lumbered into *the fence straining the wire I was worried the barbs would hurt them the posts creaking what if they? we interworked the poles between the wires ran for minutes until we felt safe laughed at ourselves he said we need a drink I've got some cider went back to he had a shed for his woodwork in a field   said welcome to the humpy I asked what said it was Australian a shanty hut rude hut   very rude only just holding up we sat in heaps woodshavings   like leaves scented   cedar he said poured some cider bottle labeled Linseed Oil tin mug we shared passed to and fro refilled it twice then he said there's another reason it's called a humpy pushed me down pulled up my t-shirt I said no no he wouldn't I scraped some sawdust from the floor blew it into his eyes called me a cow I ran home all the   stitch in my side irony taste in my mouth   those minutes seconds really held down smell of wood ragging my throat knew then what crated calves feel their utter helplessness*

i

Find me examples of irony in chapter 11 of The Secret Agent
– they are numerous. But before you begin to read, I want you
all to be clear as to what we mean and do not mean by that term.
We mean it in the strict literary sense. From the Greek *eironeia*,
meaning 'dissimulation, affected ignorance,' from which stems the
name *Eiron*, a regular character in Greek comedy, a weakling whose
only weapons are his wits and talent to deceive, irony is thus the
technique of wrong-footing the reader. It is when the ostensible
meaning of the words parts company with the intended meaning,
slides away, undermining the speaker's – and reader's – position. A
semantic slippage. But a controlled slippage, calling for a level of
mastery such as that displayed in the examples, given that you all
have the wit to find them, Watson, gum in the bin, please.

What we do not mean is the sloppy everyday use of the term to
refer to any unintended or unwanted development, as in 'ironic
twists of fate,' which are usually no more than coincidence and
bad luck, Black, such as my turning round at the wrong moment,
adopt a more normal posture, if you can. Now, questions?

Dramatic Irony? Does not differ essentially from our definition.
A character adopts a position or makes a statement which the
audience intuits to be false, deliberately so or not. Most usually
not. Bose? Where events later contradict their position? But again,
the later reversal is a controlled, carefully prepared detonation,
controlled, that is, by the plot, so as to underscore the essentially
hubristic nature of the original statement. Winslade, definition
of 'hubristic'?

Somewhat rough and ready, but near enough. Patel?

But that would assume our individual lives, or at least particular
sequences of events, are likewise dramatically plotted. Is this the
position you wish to maintain? Hammond?

Look, we are beginning to stray, intentionally I suspect, from the curricular path. Now, you have twenty minutes to locate the aforesaid passages in Conrad, starting now. In silence, please, hard though that may be for logorrhoea sufferers, Sexton. Right, time starts ... now.

My dearest, a brief brief, *written in class. (We are doing Conrad – our answer to your 'ironic German,' Thomas Mann.) From here I can see across the playing field to the horse chestnuts on the far side, and those chestnuts prompted this note.*

Do you remember our first meeting, the day before the first term, the leaves just beginning to tinge? You said you were there to acclimatise. I was just walking, savouring the peace.

I often think back to that, for I think had we first met in the Common Room at commencement of term, the chemistry of our encounter would have been subtly altered in the admixture of the others, perhaps irrevocably. And now that scares me. How fragile is our luck, our glück. *One wishes to bow in thanks.*

God knows I am not the romantic type. But you probably realize that too. Maybe not. Maybe, not knowing me otherwise, you are entirely unsurprised, unaware, how much I surprise myself, how 'out of character' I appear to myself. But what is *one's 'character?'*

All I wanted – and want – to say is a spontaneous 'thank you,' for persisting. Through the strain and drear of the winter, the belated Spring. 'Look, we have come through'. And I suddenly, and for the first time, feel secure.

I must return now to the multiple ironies of another secret agent. (Came across a poem last night. My clumsy translation: A glimpse of her shadow, her voice in the distance/ multiplies my love/ as lotus leaves fan out on a pool of jade. Bethge, I believe, but from the Chinese.)

j

- Strange pain, all down my side, like a stitch.

- Probably indigestion.

- But I didn't have any breakfast. I'm on this banana diet.

- Probably why. Try rubbing your brooch down it.

- Down what?

- Your side. It's supposed to cure colic. That's where its name comes from. Jade – Spanish for 'side,' *ijada*, because it relieves pain in the side, colic. Literally, 'colic stone.' Rub it gently up and down.

- You're winding me up.

- Look it up in the dictionary if you don't believe me. You have got a dictionary?

- Never needed one.

- If you had to earn your living…

- Believe me, I earn it. That's probably the pain. I've ricked it. You're serious?

- *Yes*. Lots of precious stones have medical uses. It's how their names were derived. Bloodstone, of course, that's obvious. Aquamarine comes from 'ague marine,' *ague* is fever. Rubies are pimples, mainly on the face, because of the colour. So you rub them with the stone.

- Like pumice?

- No, it draws them out. I'm serious. Garnet is shortened from pomegranite. It's used for bowel problems. Onyx is from 'claw' because it claws out aches in the bones, rheumatism. Jacinth for headaches - 'hyacinth.' Tourmaline for dizziness. *Tour-mal*, 'tower-sickness,' vertigo.

- You're making all this up.

- Promise you. I've been studying it. All the gemstones were codified by this mediaeval monk, a lapidarist. Like the humours. After all, we're made up of minerals. Bound to be a natural empathy. There's probably a gemstone for every ailment.

- You'd need a very large jewellery box.

- No problem for you, darling. I've never even seen that brooch before. Rupert?

- Of course.

- When did he give it to you?

- A fortnight ago. Actually, I haven't seen him since.

- Not like Rupert. So then, how did you rick your side?

- That was Jago.

- Have I met him?

- No. And you won't for a while.

- All right. I don't want your cast-offs, thank you. But I wonder where Rupert is? He was always so *keen*.

- Probably one of his trawls. He'll be back.

- You sound very sure.

- He told me how much trouble he went to to find this brooch. He wanted it exactly right, something to fit me perfectly.

- A brooch? How could a brooch *not* fit?

- He meant the stone.

- Clarissa. Do you really not know the meaning of the word 'jade'? Look, I'm going to *buy* you a pocket dictionary, advance birthday present. Leather-bound, of course. Wonder if Smythson do one? I think you can kiss Rupert goodbye.

- But he's always been so keen. But, well, tell me then.

k

Sin perhaps for some is the motivator, the necessary evil without which they could not act at all. Strange theology for many of you, maybe. But even the poet T. S. Eliot said that «it is better, in a paradoxical way, to do evil than to do nothing. At least we exist.» There may be some here today who wish the deceased had *not* existed. But to those of you bearing a grudge, let me ask you to consider whether any of us, on that sentiment, would be here, that we are all of us cut from crooked growth, and if the knot-holes in some are larger than in others, is the wood to blame? That perhaps wishing the non-existence of any creature is the greatest sin. Look instead for the redeeming acts, and pray that the evil dies with the deceased. Let the coffin be lowered.

Over, thank God, but, my God, why me? But why any? In the infinite resources of the Church there must somewhere be a line, a marker. 'Judge not,' but all living is a judging, else life's a cynicism. Unseen depths, infinite dimensions, I know, but. In any system of accounting, how does loyalty however spontaneous offset the deaths of many? Yet two women keen over his warm grave. Can they be *so* deluded? For they are more than partisan. The grief is real, sharp, the tears brim any check of dignity. One hopes to God it's from ignorance. Yet the knowledge was *there*, it was all in the public domain. I mean, it was open even to me, in my voluntary seclusion. Things I never wished to know existed in this parochial parish. Flats taken over wholesale for the growth of cannabis. Weedkiller raids on rival growers. And a more novel use for weedkiller, if rumours are true. Mixed in with the hard drugs and peddled to his challengers, anyone who crossed his path. A whisper alone would be enough. Tales of his own workers beaten to death, no chance for denial. Even if they understood the charge, if their English was adequate. Mostly Vietnamese, I believe, experienced in growing drugs but not in

English deviousness. Halfway across the world to die in a ditch. Well, if you live by the weed, you die by the wayside, I suppose, but it's a harsher truth than I've room for.

Yet is there anything sadder than a child's coffin? Smaller than a fruit crate, though more elaborate, rosewood, gilt hinges, like an expensive suitcase. Too late for the journey, though, the one that mattered. The tickets already paid for, Business Class to Atlanta, for the family of five. Who don't, to this day, know the name of their benefactor, and would be horrified to learn. Their decency might not survive it. There's an Orwellian ring about that. Decency was his highest accolade. I'm beginning to agree, now that it's harder than ever to achieve. But theirs is safe now, I think. They'll not find out the source of funding for the flight nor the course of drugs (oh, the Jesuitical irony there) to prepare for it. Only three people knew, and one is no more. His henchman (how archaic, how rustic that sounds) was scared even to tell me. And I was bound by the confessional. No, the family is safe in their ignorance. The only danger is to me.

The equations are becoming too complex today, or my brain rather is getting duller. The balance is becoming finer. Everything is becoming more nuanced.

Hate the sin and love the sinner was simplicity itself. But where does sin end and evil begin? The line is a hairline and getting finer. My eyesight can no longer cope. I've tried to thicken, coarsen the issue. To launder his reputation. But no-one else knew. To launder his soul? But he made no admission of having one, to the best of my knowledge and that of his man. No, the lines remain finedrawn.

I feel I'm dictating a letter of resignation.

Resigned, at the least, to carry on blind, to obey orders without knowing the battle. Patrol the dugouts. Carry the bandages. But succour the enemy? My terms already betray me. But I cannot pray for this man's soul. And if they wish to report me, let them. If, out of the depths of their grief, they wish to reach out at me, may it do them good.

The crowd has disappeared. Just the women left, wife and mother, clasped awkwardly together, in silhouette like a Henry Moore sculpture.

The granite against my back is hard, clean-cut despite its age. Life is rarely so symmetrical but it was in a cemetery I learned my faith. At first, the grass. The only patch of green for miles. After school and chores, to sit in the unmown margins, be still. I later began to read the headstones, tracing with a fingertip, filling in the obliterations. Subtracting dates to get the age, dividing the lifespan by my own. Multiplying, sometimes; they were the hardest, those fractions – a third, a quarter, two-fifths of fourteen. But the sense of a life, however long, wasted; a life, however fulfilled, wanting. That was the start of my faith, or search.

That and the smell of the damp, enriched with the scent of humus. Leafmould, I was told, but no, it's the scent of earthborn man, cognate, I learnt, with *inhume, exhume,* also *humility.*

But humility grows with age, with approaching inhumation as more and more seems beyond our grasp, and we give up more and more of our illusions at answers. And, from physicians of souls we end as leeches, clinging to those we can no longer cure, least of all ourselves

1

It's done, the mast stepped and gated, rigging secured, jib hoisted. Together they hoist the mainsail, Tom feeding the sail into the track while he pulls on the halyard. With the boom attached, he secures the halyard. As Tom threads the mainsheet he does the task he can perform alone.

He unrolls the spinnaker, finds the head, lays it carefully on the grass, runs his hands slowly along each of the leeches, checking for kinks, but feeling the cloth under his fingers as he does in his dreams.

He puts the foot of the sail into the bag, slowly folds in the rest, the clews overhanging the sides, the head on the top, lifts the bag over the grabrail into the boat.

Together they wheel the trolley round and down the ramp until he feels the shock of water on his legs and the boat floats free. He holds it as Tom pulls the trolley back, then pulls himself in, clips his harness line to the eyeplate.

His stomach lifts with the boat as Tom climbs aboard, hands him the jib sheet, brings the boat round. They're now sailing off the wind, almost flat-off, so he eases the sail out until it starts to luff, then brings it back in. He can feel the bite as the sail fills.

- Are we staying on a dead run?

- We will for a bit. Give her a little heel.

He holds the jib steady and leans out to windward. He hears a plane banking toward Heathrow, but he's aware only of the water running beneath him, the breeze on his face.

But it's dropping now, his hair unruffled, cheek warm. He pulls himself in, moves forward to reduce the drag, eases the jib then sheets back in.

- Once we hit halfway, we'll tack back, and set the spinnaker. Get what we can from the breeze.

He holds the sheet steady, drains his mind, only the jostle of the wind in the jib, sun on his face, free of himself.

- Coming up now.

He feels the judder as the sails luff and flap; they're facing the wind, which has risen a little. He sheets hard in, moves to aft.

- I'm bearing away slightly. Ease a little.

He eases the sheet, feels the boat respond. He's absorbed, focused on adjusting the trim to the movement of the wind, easing and sheeting almost by instinct, the jib a part of him, a wing, a fin, extrasensory.

- I'm going to hold a beam reach for a bit, then we'll beat back. There's nobody about much today. Got the reservoir to ourselves. Ready to hike.

He feels the boat pull round, right-angles to the wind. He checks his harness line, slips his feet under the straps ready to lean, but the boat's flat, the breeze settled. He relaxes into the movement, one hand skimming the water.

- I'm coming up now. Ready to tack. Okay, ready about. Watch for the boom. Oh, sorry, you know what I mean. Right. Sheet hard in. Boom's coming across now. Helm's alee.

He feels for the boom, ducks and moves across the boat, takes up the leeward sheet, pulls it hard in at first, eases off gently, leaning out against the heel.

It's a longish tack but he's on the alert. Crossing and recrossing the centreline, almost caught once by the boom, adjusting his bodyweight, thinking through his limbs and the sheet for four, now five tacks.

- I'm going to bear away now, bring her off the wind, set the spinnaker. Ease the sheet. Right. Okay, we'll sail flat-off. Step over. Hold the tiller, between your legs, haul the halyard when I yell. Hold her steady.

He hears Tom clip the pole to the mast, tenses the halyard.

- Okay, haul.

He pulls smoothly, hears the sail unfold, lift in the breeze.

- Right, I'm just cleating off the guy. Okay, I'll take her.

He steps carefully over the tiller, takes the spinnaker sheet, feeling the sail fill and pull.

- Ease out now. Okay, just beginning to curl. Sheet back in, right, ease again. That's it, trimmed nicely.

Now he can feel, respond to each shift off the breeze, an animal tautness that takes over, steadies his mind. He's found, now in his life, the ability to travel at will, through space and time. So he's no longer on a reservoir under the flight paths of Heathrow, it's salt spray he feels, riding the northeast Atlantic trades.

She's picking up speed, they both move their weight aft to lift the bow, and now they're planing, skimming the water, he feels they're flying, and the rasp of the water pistol, scald of acid, blurred red of the mailvan at last disappear, fade in the spindrift, and he's alive in the present, alive in the breeze, through the rigging, the sheet, the mast's flex and carry

m

- Already have.

- Where the hell are we going to keep a pig?

- Darling, we've acres of room. We can build a sty behind the pergola. It won't show.

- It'll smell.

- That's a myth. Pigs don't smell if they're properly looked after. It depends what you feed them on.

- And what do you feed them on?

- Mast.

- Mast?

- Beechnuts, acorns...

- Where on earth do you get those?

- The children can collect them in the park.

- Are they allowed to?

- Who's going to stop them?

- But that's in the autumn. What about now?

- Apples, vegetables, kitchen scraps. And they dig up worms.

- Dig up the lawn? Why couldn't you have got chickens? Everyone's going in for chickens these days.

- Exactly.

- Of course. You just have to go one better. What are you going to do with it?

- *Do?*

- Chickens give eggs. What do pigs give?

- Bacon, of course.

- Marigold, you have to kill it first. Who's going to do that? You?

- You're the man of the house.

- Oh no. Leave me out. The children already think me an ogre for having that fox-cub put down. You'll have to get in a professional slaughterman. There must be some. Look in Yellow Pages. Or Farmers' Weekly. My God, it's like something from the war. Then people clubbed together to buy one, took it in turns to feed it. This one will be all down to me.

- If expense is all that's worrying you, we'll have it in place of our next holiday.

- I'm not forgoing my week in Verbier for the sake of a pig, thank you. And I can't see the children doing so, either. If you wish to stay at home...

- Don't be so stuffy. Besides, wartime practices are all the fashion now. Make Do And Mend. Dig For Victory. Allotments. Even after the war, Mummy used to tell me as a girl they put all their leftovers into a pigbin, and a lorry came round once a week to collect it for swill.

- You'll do the same, I suppose? Go round all the neighbours, 'please save us your swill.' We have a perfectly good Farmers' Market in Richmond.

- Doing it oneself is so much more satisfying.

- You won't be doing it yourself, not the hard part. And by then, the children will be too attached to it, like the fox-cub.

- Maybe we could breed it instead.

- Is it male or female?

- I didn't ask.

- Marigold, you haven't thought this through at all, have you? It's not one of those Pot-Bellied Siamese things, is it?

- Of course not. A proper English pig. A Gloucester Old Spot.

- When are they delivering it?

- As soon as I let them know the sty's ready.

- Who's actually constructing this sty?

- I've asked that little man who did the children's grotto. He's going to shuffle a few jobs round, prioritise it. May up the price a little. But I'm sure I can knock him down.

- Well, you've certainly knocked me down. Last thing I expected over lunch. What on earth possessed you?

- I've always wanted one. Don't know why. Actually I think I do know why. They're so, dependable. Rubs off onto their keepers. Eumaeus was my very favourite character in the Odyssey.

Reading Classics at Royal Holloway, I was going out with Johnny Pendleton – you don't know him – thorough bastard he turned out to be. One of my friends called him a swine, and I said, No, that's just what he's not.

- What's so dependable about pigs? Dogs, yes.

- I've always thought so. When we were little, my brother had a farmyard in the nursery. You know, farmhouse, tractor, figures. And a pigsty with a black and white pig, lying down. Whenever Mummy and Dadds were having a sticky patch, I'd go up to the nursery, close the door and watch the pig, and it seemed so, idyllic, *bucolic*.

- Bucolic comes from *boukolos*, a cowman. I suppose I should think myself lucky you didn't want to play milkmaids.

- No. Only pigs. They're gentle, safe ...

- Marigold? Marigold what's the matter? What on earth is it? Here, have a nip of my malt. Look, I've said you can have it.

n

carried to his right, which is unusual, you normally slip the strap over your right shoulder, so the case hangs on your left. Should have made me suspicious, but I assumed he was left handed. Or maybe ambidextrous, like me, only mine's training. I normally have to work with my left hand, across my body. - What? - No, my arm inside my raincoat. I've got vents in the seams below the armhole. - Well, I only work wet rush hours. - I lean across, holding a newspaper in the other hand, slit the side of the case, slide out the notebook, slip in a book of about the same weight, bulldog clip the slit, done.

 - What? Yeah, textbook m.o. except all seemed too easy.

 - Well, *course* I'm admitting to theft. - Because the charge I'm facing is worse. Lot worse. - No I don't think I was followed. I'd have noticed. - Because I'm a fuckn professional. - Alright, sorry. No, it must've had a pigeon in it. - A homer, a microchip. I usually check, only I never had time. I'd hardly got indoors when they arrived. Asked for their search warrants, said they weren't there to search, just ask a few questions. Picked up the computer straight away, asked if it was mine. Naturally I said yes. - Well I'd hardly tell them I'd stolen it, would I? - Not straight off. But when they booted it, started pulling all these porn shots from the hard drive, course I tried to tell them the truth. Too late then. Christ, you should have seen some of the shots. Barely five years old, some of them. Felt sick looking at them. - Look, I'm not a nonce, right? - Don't quote laws to me, that's your job. Look, you've got to get me off. - Defence? I was set up for this. That's your defence, that's your angle. - Because they get more points for a paedo than a nip. Obvious. - Show them my raincoat, tools. - Okay, I'll admit to previous offences, if necessary. - Yeah, prove I'm a professional. - It's still better than this. It's not just prison. My contacts, my girlfriend, my whole fuckn *life* goes down the sewer. You *have* to get the charges altered. - Because even without a jury, even in a closed court, it's gonna be hard to get off. - They've got ways. It's worse than you think. Look, I told you I'm not a nonce, but. Some of those shots, Christ. Not the real kids, but a couple of the older ones. One especially. Haunts me, gives me the sweats. - I guess twelve, thirteen, but. The orbs she had on her. - No, not her eyes. The body of a seventeen year old. You'd never have - Know what scares me? Suppose they wire me up to a brain scanner, show all these shots again. Ball and chain rest of

O

the threshold of the old Town Hall, *la Mairie, oui?* Now, you have already seen the new town hall, when the Mayor greeted you all yesterday. But this was, for many years, *la Mairie*, until it became too small, and the lovely new one was built, out of town, at which time this one became an Arts Centre. Sadly, there was no art to fill it, so after standing empty for some time, it was turned into, as you can see, *un bistro*, a um... pub. Sorry?   Yes, almost next door to another pub, and indeed, a licensed club on the other side. The pub you allude to is in fact, very historic, dating back to the thirteenth century, and was, until a few years ago, an hotel as well as bar.   *Les fenêtres,* the windows, *oui?* Well spotted. Yes. Some of the upper windows are actually picture windows, I mean pictures *of* windows, painted on top of the bricks, the false windows. The brick windows would be known architecturally as orbs, from the Latin *orbus*, meaning 'bereft, deprived,' of one's parents, for instance, or in this case, deprived of light, sightless, blind windows, blank panels.

Although, strictly speaking perhaps, these do not qualify as orbs, as they were not installed as such. No, they were originally proper windows, only later bricked up.   Why? Because many years ago, the government imposed a tax on windows, and rather than pay so much tax, people bricked up as many windows as they could spare.

No no, not *Marguerite* Thatcher, *non.* William the Third, in the seventeenth century. And increased, I'm sorry to tell you, during the Napoleonic Wars. There are other examples in the town I can show you later.

Dark Ages? Well, yes. But I suppose good news for candle makers. It's an ill wind, as we say here, that blows nobody any good. Sad, though. The windows are the eyes of a house, even a public house *blank   blank stare always his response shutter   blind come down shut out sure he couldn't help wanted to explain promised promised to explain always later older when you're promised eyes limp the scars nightscreams asking prompting made up stories always a blank complicated he'd hard to explain details I'd grenade but German? not German long journey home I felt I feel a right to years of my life leading him round try touch his Brailled face shy shy away feel the warmth my fingers perhaps his promise told me he'd told it put it on tape but after his death but then after his death after the had to rewind old reel-to-reel like shuttles then blank wiped blank*

Sad, *n'est-ce pas?* Yes, curtains painted on the shutters. Very clever, *trompe-l'oeil, oui?* Now, across here we have our town War Memorial. You have one in Melun?

When the market place was pedestrianised and cobbled, the memorial was cleaned and the names recut. Clearly incised in the stone. You can trace them with your fingers. Some of the names were added after the last war, but most of them are from the First War. What stories each of these names could tell, *non?* From a time when stories could still be told.

Yes, *oui,* horror stories in many cases. But each one had his own story, a fragment of the mosaic of history. A *tessera* I believe is the correct term. Although many of the stories will have been lost to history, or marginalised by the scholars, I'm sure they live on in family memory, in both our lands. Partly, that's why we're here today, isn't it, our bond of history. And these exchange visits, aren't they valuable? They allow us to get to know each other's history not just on the national level but on the individual, the personal. Similar, I understand - I've been swotting up, as we say - to the distinction you make between *langue* and *parole,* the river of the French language and your own personal dips in and from it. Sorry? You don't... comprehend? Ah. You're not familiar with French structuralist ideas? Well, never mind. We'll look at a few more English structures, in the High Street, then I think it will be time for tea.

Oui, yes, the Mayor will be there. *Mon mari? Non,* no, he's not my husband, *non.* I have no *mari.* No, never. Now, we turn right into the High Street. This too, you'll notice, is pedestrianised. It is now where we hold the market, instead of the market square. Well, because there's more room. Next month we will be hosting a French market again. Yes, the traders are all French, *oui.* Oh, baskets, rush mats, food, of course. *Fromages, oui. Pain,* yes, all kinds of bread. *Beaucoup de pains always the pain*

p

of my life. I just can't risk that. You've gotta get the charge changed.   -   Whatever. But even with previous, at least I'll get parole. But on this hook, forget it.   -   Get me off?   -   Yeah, I know you are, that's why I'm calling you, but your middle name's not Christ, is it, and that's what it would take   -   Look, I had the laptop on me, I admitted it was mine.   -   By mistake? My reaction to the paedo shots? Pretty bloody smashed out, to start with. But they probably weren't looking at my reactions, too busy gawping at the bloody images themselves. And when they were watching me, that's when, I told you, some of the later ones, they were really getting to me. They'd have noticed that, alright. No, it's all too risky.

   -   I can't risk going down on this one.   -   It's not that. I can take care of myself, even in there. No, I'll tell you what scares me. Having my life fucked. Because I'll have lost Maria, for good, depend on it. And what'll keep me warm inside? Those paedo shots. Some of them, I told you. But maybe even some of the others, the really young ones'll start to get to me. And when I do get out, what woman's going to have me? Give a dog a name, he might as well live up to it. And all those months, years, of thinking, leching, I'm going to *be* a fuckn paedo.   -   Well, could you at least try and get bail?   -   Yeah, I can pull something together.   -   Because I reckon my only chance is to skip, get the first plane out of Heathrow.

p

The tree, a plane, one of many surrounding the green, a smooth paper-grained bark, lichen-bossed, silvery green in the filtered light, has its trunk punctuated at head height by a rectangle of white smooth-grained paper.

A man's head under a baseball cap, the face's sharp features blunted, smudged by the grainy resolution of photocopy corruption.

Below the head, two blocks of text.

HAVE YOU SEEN MY HUSBAND? I JUST WANT HIM TO KNOW THAT I LOVE HIM AND WANT HIM BACK. PLEASE HELP ME IF YOU CAN.

CZY KTOŚ WIDZIAŁ MOJEGO MĘŻA? TYLKO CHCĘ MU POWIEDZIEĆ, ŻE GO KOCHAM I CHCĘ BY DO MNIE WRÓCIŁ PROSZĘ POMÓŻ JEŚLI MOŻESZ.

Common to both texts, a phone number, numeric Esperanto, a lynchpin of trust.

Already, nightdew and rain have wrinkled the paper, the disintegration of hope foreshadowed in the ruck, the tears …

r

story before, on the Roman finds of the county archaeologists, before the extraction began, but this is older, deeper, literally deeper, below, before, the layer of the dig, unearthed in the gravel layers beneath the clay. He picks his way between the rucks, feet sliding in the shifting gravel, until he reaches the conveyor belt, inert for now, and firm ground, more aware now of the rucks towering behind him, modern ziggurats, pyramids, he thinks, but transient, more like dunes, shifting, reconfigured by the lorries and conveyor. He's apprehensive, unsure of his ground. Roman bricks and pottery are within imaginative ken, but this? He's wishing they'd sent the photographer with him. (Why pictures of a level-crossing? That body is gone. This body is here.)

He leaves the conveyor, walks to the bulldozed ridges of the outer workings. There it is, like a four-poster bed in a field (wasn't that Auden? Spender?) - metal stakes with a tarpaulin cover. It's not been systematically dug yet, the archaeologists haven't started, and he probably shouldn't be here, but he wanted to look for himself, by himself, before it was all clinically exposed like an outdoor morgue. To get his own reactions, raw.

He spreads his handkerchief on the ground, kneels under the canopy. He feels a chill despite the heat, the vent of time, the ages falling away beneath him.

He can make out, in the shade of the cover and in the caked clay, the skull, an arm, a foot, what looks like the remains of a hide quiver with a few flint arrowheads. How long have they been here? He assumes them to be Neolithic, he's not sure, but maybe five, six thousand years? He tries to get some grasp on that, converting it into generations. Divide by seventy, gives eighty, approximately. Eighty life-spans. But wouldn't the average life-span shorten as you went backwards? A mediaeval span was maybe forty. In *his* time, what? Thirty? Less?

It doesn't help, anyway. He tries instead to picture the scene as *he* would have encountered it, blot out the planes overhead, the railway across the field, imagine the silence. But maybe it was noisier then, others calling, children shouting, birds, the cry of game. Was this forest, pasture, scrub? He has no idea.

He gives up, attempts to jot down a few heads. He can't write the story until he interviews the archaeologists, which he decides to do over the phone from the office. But maybe the caption.

'Barrowboy Exposed.' But was this a barrow? Was it even a grave? By the angle of the arm and foot, he guesses this is where he died, trapped, tripped, drowned? Murdered? Was he hunting or hunted? Maybe work in a play on quarry/gravel pit?

But it all feels inadequate as a response to the body, the abyss. He tries again to make that empathetic leap, attempt some bond.

Suddenly he misses his wife in a way that's new to him. He needs the foreshortening of the present, the warmth.

He owes it to the corpse to make one last attempt, forces himself to reach out, touch the flintheads, quiver

q

door that swings easily, closes with a whisper, and importantly, will admit his girth and hold-all without struggle, the room light and cool, the pastel walls unobtrusive yet, though he's not keen on apricot, not the bland off-white or ivory of most short-stay hotels. And there's a reassuring quiver to the mattress as he pulls back the duvet, pats the bed with his hand, although the real test will come tonight, 'tested to destruction,' the phrase goes. It still makes him smile, and so does the job, he's not got over it yet, never thought he'd have the nerve even to attend the interview, look on the lads's faces when he'd told them he'd been called in. Their idea, applying, big joke round the depot, he didn't mind, could take a joke, case of having to, 'Col's a sport, at least he can take a joke,' and they'd said 'What are you going to wear, Col?' and he'd replied 'Don't worry, I've got a suit, and at least I won't have to fill in the bloody forms for every new uniform, with the measurements in triplicate,' all the same, when he got there, waiting with six other applicants, he'd thought, Sod it, why not? and pitched it to the interview team behind their glass desk, said, Well if you really want a thorough test, it has to be in beyond-normal conditions, as in engineering, and he thinks he even used that phrase, 'tested to destruction,' and two of them had turned to each other, eyebrows raised, which he'd taken as a dismissal but they asked him to wait out the rest of the interviews then called him back in, offered him the job, and he'd gone back to the depot there and then, still in his suit, then stood them all drinks in the pub after work, thanking them slyly for the suggestion.

Only two months but a lifetime ago.

There's an armchair beside the bed, wooden armrests but fairly wide, he lowers himself in, tight fit but more comfortable than sitting on the bed, at least he can lean back, pulls the hold-all over, takes out the notebook, jots down remarks on reception, decor, door and chair, silently laughing his enjoyment of the undercover aspect, looks at his watch. Will he still make it for lunch? How long do they serve? How *large* do they serve? He's had to order extra dishes, extra *meals* in some places, they've already queried his expenses for the first month, now he pays for the extras himself, tries to do without if he can, an economy-controlled diet, must remember that one for when he next meets the lads, though it's not as good as the 'staple diet' one, when he'd had the operation, though they wore it to death when he came out of hospital, used it for months, Still on your staple diet, Col?, offered him paper clips at tea break. Petered out though, as the weight returned and the surgeons wouldn't attempt it again. He wonders now how different his life would have been if it had worked, no different probably, still at the depot, might never have thought of applying for this job, a dream job, paid to travel, a dream come true, always longed to travel but, the awkwardness, the looks, had to pay for two seats once, never travelled after that. Now he's being professionally awkward, he feels no embarrassment, it's unbelievable, just convert any harassment into a paragraph in his report, all becomes business, no longer personal. But sometimes, just sometimes, he'd like it to be personal, travelling by himself, it's like a permanent holiday, that's what they'd all said to him, but to holiday alone, how many of them would, but he wouldn't let on, so maybe, just maybe, if the staples had worked his life would be different, you never know, but you never know what's round the corner, he's meeting more people now than he ever met at the depot, who knows, now his luck's in, every day new places, new faces, but he must get down to lunch, pushes himself up by the armrests, reminds himself to ask to keep the menu along with the bill, an *aide mémoire* for the morning when he converts it all into points, assesses where to place the hotel on the scale.

S

Opens on the 13th. of next month? Yes, I believe I knew that.
- Oh, I suppose so. Support our laddies, yes, switch on, watch
them scale the ladder, flex the board. - Yes, nervewracking.
My own wee trick was to stare into the water, try to penetrate it,
d'you see, focus on the tiles below. Helped me concentrate, stops
the butterflies. - Coaching? No, I've never coached. When
my career was over, I just wanted to get out, do something else.
- Anything, at the time. - Yes, a lot of people said that, put
something back into the sport, bring on the new generation. Oh,
I felt the force of the argument, yes, but somehow I, well, I just
didn't feel I could take responsibility for someone else's life. I
couldn't explain it, not then. - Now? Well, maybe let's just say
I think I understand, myself, but it wouldn't explain anything to
another. Still, I can truly say that I gave of my best in my own
career. Although of course it wasn't a career, in those days, not
the way you think. All strictly amateur, then. Had to go before a
committee sometimes to prove it. Expenses, time off work for
training, if you were lucky, time off for the Games, again if you
were lucky, some of them had to use their holiday. I remember
one poor laddie, one of the rowers, I believe, worked for Cable
& Wireless. Refused him leave, said he'd already used it all up.
Not even the Prime Minister could get them to relent. So I was
lucky in that, at least. - Not so lucky there, no. America pretty
well dominated the pool then, too. In the springboard, it was a
straight one, two, three for them, and in the highdive they took
gold and silver, Germany the bronze. Well, that's how it goes.
But it's competing that's important. We really believed that then.
That's why we found the whole ethos there puzzling, almost
repugnant, some of us, the idea of winning at all costs, of proving
your country's supremacy, no, we didn't really understand that,
we were there to compete, do our best, and enjoy ourselves. -

Patriotic, of course we were. But we weren't political, really. That rather washed over our heads. And we were all very young, d'you see, left all the politics to the officials. - Aware of the boycott movement, obviously. But again, that wasn't, we felt, a question for us. It had all been voted on, decided, we were selected, off we went to do our best. - Over there? Well, we came up against it, but we felt, *I* felt, rather, that I wouldn't allow it to upset my focus. I didn't understand all the currents, the eddies. I mean, for example, in the Olympic Village, all the houses were named after German towns, and we, the British - the men, that is; the lassies had their own accommodation, nearer the stadium - our houses were all named after Rhineland towns. And I just thought, well, they're German towns, after all, they may have a right to be there. That was the limit of my thinking then. I was still in my teens, remember. And we were all quite impressed by the village itself, clean, modern, spick and span, good food, plenty of it. They'd gone to a lot of trouble. And no swastikas in the village itself, by the way. - Naive? Oh aye, you could say so. But hindsight's a gift not bestowed on the young, so they say. You have to take as you find. - I found the ordinary people friendly enough, helpful, certainly. We were told later that they'd been ordered to be friendly, and happy too. For the Olympic fortnight there was compulsory cheerfulness. But it wasn't all done to order. I mean, Jesse Owens, for example. The crowds, the ordinary Germans, loved him. Everywhere you'd hear them chanting, Yessir, Yessir, Yessir Ovens - No, no, the ovens came later, of course. The blessings of hindsight again, d'you see. I'm trying to remember it as we saw it at the time. - Certainly, the saluting and heiling struck me as sinister. But I heard it argued by some of the athletes that it was simply applying the discipline of sport to society. I didn't really go along with that, of course. Very different from the British tradition of muddling through. And sport to me was *self*-discipline, no more. But all that was, shall I say, the backdrop, the scale of it all removed it from our focus. No, it was the little things that got through to us. There were rumours that the German divers had extra practice time, at night, that they had had government training facilities, extended leave, and so forth. That's what upset us a little. Although I didn't allow it to upset me, personally. - The note, I suppose. - I've never spoken about this before. A note, left in my blazer pocket. - The pool had wooden cubicles for us to change in. I suppose while I was diving, someone sneaked the note in, hid it in my inside pocket. I didn't find it for a while. I wasn't in the habit of carrying a wallet in those days. Precious little to keep in it. Money I kept in my trouser pocket. - It was quite short, very odd. I didn't know what to make of it. - It started off, I remember, 'After these Games, our life will «resume.»'. Then a remark about ancestry, 'my ancestry be recovered,' 'the ground trembles like the springboard on my feet, but I cannot to swim …' - Yes, odder and odder. It ended, 'please to consider me when you travel to England, to journey as your guest.' Well. I took it at first as a hoax. - Exactly. And yet... Each team had an army officer attached. Ours was obviously not one for pranks. But we also had boys assigned to us, in some sort of youth service - yes, in uniform. They were there to run errands, post letters for us, act as guides, be generally helpful. Bit like Bob-a-Job Week. One of them, timid laddie, I used to catch him staring at me. I've often wondered since if maybe it was him. But what could I have said? - Nothing. I thought of showing it to our coach, but, suppose it made trouble? So I left it in my pocket. - No, I never heard. Nor after the war. Strange, I've not really thought about it until lately. You know, as you get older, you live more in the past. And the future. Parts of your past become more vivid. And your possible futures, I mean, your deaths, likewise. - Well, you don't want a maudlin interview with an old man. Where were we? Oh aye, yes, I'll be watching with interest, spurring them on, so if you can pass on my support. - Happy to oblige.

cannot to swim he'll have found his waterwings by now was it Kingsley? water babies but how will it be for me have I lost my touch my timing which stance

68

to adopt upright if I'm in my bed in the wheelchair'd be a tuck then what reverse somersault with double rotation with time aplenty to straighten out through to the ankles pierce the water with the barest ripple a perfect ten and the water stinging is that how it will be but without the light the dazzle the applause breaking the surface into a refracted a translated world or will it be just the dive continued to infinity into a clinging dark free of distraction the wheelchair the solicitous hands or the hands hand holding me back losing my stance on the board a final ignominious bellyflop is that how an amateurish splash at the last and will he be there whoever he was acclimatised already a local lad again act as my guide tow me through the underworld

t

Would surprise them, he thinks, if they knew, his family, the village. All fretting at him flitting off to London, fetching after a girl, and here he is, quietly following his trade, same as ever.

He lifts the sheep up over the fence, careful of the barbs, stands it on its feet, checks for injury. Sets off to find the gap in the fence. Could be anywhere in its length, but he's sure the sheep hadn't been over there long. He walks slowly, looking for lambs that might have followed, as well as the gap. He can make out a fleck of wool low on the fence, heads toward it.

He's right. He pulls the tow from the twist of wire, releases it to the breeze, stoops to the hole. It's a size. He takes the skein of orange nylon from his pocket, criss-crosses the gap, but it's makeshift, it needs a proper darn. First he needs to check the inner fence, ringing the reservoir, just to make sure. He walks on to the next trestle, vaults the fence, walks up the incline, steeper now, to the fence on the water's edge. He walks back along it, checking by sight and tension, but it seems intact. The light off the water dazzles, he pulls his cap down over his eyes. But he's soothed by the lap of the waves. Like the sea, he thinks, except for the planes. He makes an effort not to look up as one now lifts above the far bank, as if emerging from the water, slowly rolls and turns.

Satisfied as to the fence, he half slithers down to the outer fence, back over the trestle, sets off to his hut for tools and wire.

It's hot. He's tempted to have his lunch and drink first, but decides against it. He'd rather see the job done, then it's not on his mind. Him all over, as they used to say, and he's surprised himself to find himself here, all this way on what seemed like a whim, but a whim only from the outside, not something to be explained and he didn't try.

He sorts out wirecutters, pliers and a reel of wire, walks back to where the gap was. He kneels, cuts the nylon carefully and rewinds it, then cuts out the rusted wire, unreels the galvanized and twists the end firmly into the bottom lateral with the pliers. He estimates the length, cuts it, weaves it through the mesh of the fence, ties it in, cuts and weaves another length. Whole fence should be renewed, galvanized throughout, never allow a rusted fence like that at home, but here he's only a hired hand, an employee. The word makes him smile, he's talking Town. Having to learn. Your bloody language, Velta says, how should I understand you? We must both learn proper English from my books. He's learning it mostly from newspapers. He tests the fence, pulling the darn as hard as he can. It seems secure.

He carries the tools back to his hut, takes his lunchbox over to the hawthorns, sits in the shade. The side of his hut, from where he sits, is sharply defined, a sort of sundial. There were old men in the village who claimed they could tell the time from the shadow of trees. He believes them but why bother, watches are cheap. Life is changing. Cold pizza in his lunchbox. Velta brought it back from her work last night.

He tosses the crust to the sparrows in the hawthorn. The cider's warm. He decides to get his rod from the hut, do a little angling for an hour, cool the cider at the same time. Now shearing's over he can afford to relax a little, they won't need dagging for a while, until the fleece grows back. He's folded a few that were cut in shearing, so he can watch for flystrike, but he can check them later.

He puts his empty lunchbox in his hut, takes out the old one he's filled with sawdust and the maggots he's taken from the sheep, and his rod and net, picks up the cider.

He walks the long way round to the perimeter gate. There's a decline, a natural ditch where sheep are in the habit of getting stogged, but it's a reflex action, there's no danger until they're fully fleeced again, and the ditch is dry anyway. But he likes to be methodical, keep to routine.

He unlocks the gate, across the footpath and he's onto the

moor. There's the constant boom of traffic from the M25 but as he pushes through the undershrub he can blot it out, listen to the river instead. It's full, quick, despite the dry spring, reminds him of the brooks back home. No brownies here though, but he's hoping for umber, they're just as good, as sport and as good to eat. A couple of two-pounders, get Velta to cook them, sprig of thyme to bring out the flavour, eat them cold. He scans the water for the tell-tale fin. He throws in a few maggots, watches. A small shoal of dare take them as they sink, shimmy away. He catches a flash of greygreen, didn't spot the fin but it's worth a hope. He checks his hook, tests the cast, baits up with a pair of maggots. Back home he'd dryfly for umber but it looks too uppy down here, only coarse angling, he's noticed, but he's happy with that.

He slides the float down six inches, casts carefully toward the reeds upstream, now he's concentrating on the red tip of the quill, forgets all else, even the planes.

u

if it comes off, if not, not. One last throw. Clear decks of all
Colour Theories, vapid Kandinskian crap, Spiritual Abstraction
(Newman's zips of enlightenment, Rothko's zipless fucks).
Alternatives?

(i) Total randomness (?) Kelly. Richter.

Richter scale   earthquakes.   mudslides.   Burnt Umber   Raw
Sienna   Naples Yellow.   Earth of one's birthplace.
Aboriginal art - colour <u>is</u> the pigment   pigment <u>is</u> the meaning.
(But the bastards sold out, all use acrylics now).

So

(ii) Total subjectivity. Autobiographical, not aesthetic,
choices. Mix own pigments where possible.   (back to basics.
pre-Pre-Raphaelite. every self-respecting artist ground his own
colours. we've become effete)

Explore.

Ochre ground - gravel pit clay (Raw Staines)
(suburban anonymity)   Linseed oil suspension, overall wash.
(Traffic soot for Lamp Black?)

Streaks of Cobalt (mining the self - dangerous. Rilke?
confront the mountain demons) Cobalt is corrosive!

A ritual exorcism (childhood ghosts) - smouldered birch
(gives Brown Bistre)

Stain of Golden Alison (fugitive - all the better)

Grass green - colour of happiness (stains on her skirt).
Find a Sap green, to overlay.

Red? traditionally from cochineal insects. Substitute - bed
bugs? (do Bohemian shit-holes still exist? must do somewhere).
spots of blood red   (hers or mine?)

Verdigris = wine dregs on copper (find some copper)

Indigo? use woad   traditionally, covered with piss and trampled   (galleries, critics, whole fucking industry)

Madder   Mediterranean areas only. Native substitute - Dodder? (also more apt)

Binder - simple linseed. Permanence not important (NO POSTERITY).   More unstable the better. Photograph when finished then leave to degrade. (An art of <u>de</u>composition) Therefore: no assemblages, no collages, no spatchcocked vamps.

<u>The purity of decay.</u>

V

will be ready for you tomorrow. No, I'll make sure of it, even if I have to work on them this evening. Not often I get the chance to handle shoes of this quality round here. I mean, look, the cut-out on the vamps. Exquisite. Glacé kid, from a glance. Am I right? Yes, long while since I've had shoes like this brought in. Should have relocated to Richmond, or Old Windsor, but it's the capital, of course. And the upheaval. Need to do it while you're still young, if you do it at all.

Well, I get by, you know, bread and butter work still coming in, resolings, stretchings, although the advent of trainers didn't help. Never mind. Take the rough with the smooth, the bunions with the Louboutins, though round here it's mostly the former. Hence, as you can see, I've had to diversify. Pompom slippers, lightweight luggage. All tat really. No, mustn't be snobbish. Sort of stuff I grew up with. Just happened to have an aunt who married well, moved to Walton, by the river. Used to go and stay, be coddled, as she put it.

She used to have dinner parties. I'd sneak in and under the table before the guests arrived. That's what sparked my interest in shoes - I'd try to match the shoes to the voices, to begin with. Then the shoes themselves became the fascination. I'd resist for a while, then catch myself stroking them. Sometimes they'd jerk their foot, and I realized that some leather was so fine they could feel my fingertips. My first lesson in quality.

I couldn't emerge until after they'd gone, so I couldn't see their faces, but I found I didn't need to, the shoes were enough. Then I'd go round the table emptying the glasses, stagger to my room, intoxicated by it all.

No, never really thought about it. It wasn't an option round here in those days. Maybe if I'd been brought up in the East End, where there's a local tradition. Incidentally, that's how I came to propose to my wife. She brought in the most gorgeous pair of Ginas, chequerboard design in gold embossed leather and cream calfskin, square-toed, bark-tanned soles, wooden heels needed retipping.

When she called back for them, I mentioned to her that despite the Italian label and being named after Lollobrigida, they were actually made in Dalston. She looked so crestfallen. Then she laughed. That was the moment I decided to propose. After a suitable courtship.

Oh, the treasures she had. Rainbow-toed black Mary Janes by Jourdan, green-and-beige Cuban-heeled Cardins, pink satin pumps with diamanté band by Vivier. Even a pair of Ferragamos, black satin evening sandals, sling backs with interlaced vamp and stiletto heel made from a hollow brass cage. Heirlooms, I assumed, they weren't her size, neither was she old enough, though she was of a certain age.

The way she treated her shoes, though. Some beginning to crease, even crack. She'd come in, kick them off, leave them wet. I was forever scurrying round putting in the trees, polishing, bringing them back to scratch while she poured the drinks. She did it deliberately, I'm sure. I suspect she even scuffed them on purpose. Stiil, small price to pay.

God, here's me gabbling on, taking your time. Now, that's a resole, heels retipped, and I'll rub in a beeswax restorative overnight, final spit and polish in the morning, good as new. How about a new inner sole? Have they stretched at all? Just slip them on a sec.

Oh yes, proportion of toe cleavage, perfect. They've retained their fit. Well yes, that's always a hazard for the devoted, shoes do leave weals.

w

I silence the most boisterous of guests with one of my looks. I don't think we need worry, Robin. And even the most remote of republics are perfectly civilized close up. Where were we? '… My husband and I have always had the keenest interest not only in the Commonwealth but indeed the common weals of all nations …' *Is* there a plural of 'weal,' Robin?

- On the analogy of 'musics,' ma'am. Just as societies have very different musical cultures, so do nations have very different resources of wealth. In this case, mostly mineral, gas and oil. Plus the odd bale of cotton.

- It sounds rather high-falutin. Did Number 10 suggest it? Anthony is rather keen on such new-fangled speech, one observes. Very well, we'll accede. Let us just hope the President of Turkmenistan knows no better. I believe, by the way, he has yet to arrive. What's the e.t.a. at W.C.?

- Ma'am?

- Windsor Castle, Robin. One of Charles' usages. Apparently.

- Flight touches down Heathrow 4.57, arrival Windsor 5.45, perambulatory drinks 6.20, normal order of events from 7.

- Oh for a long soak and the new Dick Francis, Robin. One sometimes wonders, if it hadn't been for That Woman … But here we are. Now. Let us not dawdle. '… world grows increasingly smaller … ever greater mingling of common interests … pooling of resources, with closer links forged through trade… Our nation has much to offer her partners… inventiveness … Great Britain has the X-Factor.' Explain that for me, Robin. One likes to understand the jokes one makes.

- It's a t.v. programme, ma'am.

- A televised treasure hunt?

- Actually a talent show.

- Why 'X-factor'?

- X is that indefinable ingredient. You know, like the 'It-girl.'

- I'm not sure I do know, Robin. Is it any good?

- I'm told it's very popular, ma'am.

- Perhaps one should watch it. Encourage new enterprise. Does it clash with Inspector Morse, or my husband's Celebrity Wife Swap?

- I wouldn't know, ma'am.

- Maybe we'll ask the page to alter channels one week. Where were we? Yes. Turkmenistan is Muslim. Remind me to remind my husband to have a whisky *before* collecting the President. Now, '… Britain has the X-Factor, your nation has the Gas-Factor …' No, no, Robin, this really won't do. The popular touch, in the right context, but really. How is the poor President to follow all this? Do they even have television in Turkmenistan?

X

Where am I hoping to take this? All the way, to the top of the league, why not? Aim high. I know this is only hospital radio, not the BBC, but I want this to be as professionally run as possible. So it's important for you to get the pronunciation right, master the more common shibboleths of the language, set an example to both staff and patients. I don't want ethnic excuses. The best English is spoken in India. Why not also in Ashford and St. Peter's?

Besides, if we can prove a degree of excellence in broadcasting, we can claim a grant under the Government's English Outreach Initiative. So there you are. Principle and lucre combined. Odd, incidentally, that 'lucre' now carries a pejorative connotation, when its root meaning is neutral - gain or profit. Odder still that the connotation still obtains when profit is so highly esteemed. But we're digressing.

Now, a few preliminary vulgarisms to avoid. Let's start at the end, alphabetically, and work backward, just for novelty. Novelty leaves a deeper impression, I find. We'll begin with 'Xmas,' which is never, ever, pronounced 'Ex-mas' except by the illiterate. It's not an X, it's the Greek *Khi*, the initial letter of *Khristos*, Christ. Hence, *Christ*mas. And while we're on the subject of carols, it's 'God Rest Ye Merry, Gentlemen,' (comma after 'Merry', not 'Rest') but in the phrase Ye Olde Tea Shoppe, in case of rare need, it's not *Yee*, but *The*, not a Y but the equivalent of the now obsolete letter for our *th*.

I know there are five months until the festive season, but by the time we've worked backwards, then forwards again, it'll be upon us.

On the subject of abbreviations: VIZ is the name of a comic; 'viz,' short for *videlicit*, meaning *namely*, is pronounced 'namely.' And while we're in the Vs, it's *vic͞e versa*, and *víola* for the flower, *vióla* for the instrument.

You might be thinking all this is pedantic, yes? But what does 'pedantic' mean? From the Italian *pedante*, it just means 'a teacher.' Again , it's acquired a pejorative use. Governments stress the importance of education, but society demeans those who try to educate, or educate themselves. And ultimately, all education is self-education.

Let me tell you something. I was a working-class lad, local Grammar boy. Lessons were water off a duck's back. One day we had to take turns reading aloud. One boy, Jones, never forgotten him, pronounced 'meringue' *mering-you*. Whole class laughed, maliciously, me included, even though I'm sure some of us knew no better. I thought about that. I was determined never to be laughed at, looked down on, by anyone. Correctness is equality. That's true for everyone. It's true for new arrivals, ethnic minorities. Linguistic equality is the first step to self-assertion, self-confidence.

But there's another reason for all this. Cosmologists talk about wormholes in space, short-cuts to other universes. Words are wormholes in time. Etymology is archaeology. Language is the pool of all the chance encounters of the past. Everything leaves its trace. Strike a musical note, listen hard and you can hear a whole series of overtones, forming the resonance of the note. Words carry their own overtones, the history of their usages. They resonate. Life becomes richer. Culture grows. Bacteria in a dish, that's a culture, multiplying, expanding. We belong. All of us. We add to the present by our past. we contribute by our background. You too. Especially you. Every visitor, every immigrant, every migrant worker. Each Polish plumber leaves his trace, like Huguenot jewellers and Flemish merchants, as much as Roman legions and Norman soldiers. It's in language that they live on. And language is how we find ourselves as individuals, how we live on. Linguistic correctness is how we honour the dead, and each other.

I'm getting carried away here. I know it's just a hospital radio, not the World Service. But it's at the local level that standards can be held, and where the bacteria grows. It's the Indian newsagent and the Polish builder, not the Indian or Polish ambassadors, who enrich the language. In time, maybe *chuti* and *jaldi jaldi* will be as familiar as *wallah* and *shampoo*. Or *zloty* for 'vending machine.'

I know, it's a sad fact. Many borrowings embed a history of friction rather than friendship. Even 'refugee,' or *refugie*, came in with the Huguenots, who were not exactly welcomed with open arms, in England at least.

But it works both ways. Take 'Yank,' short for 'Yankee,' and derived from *Janke*, the Dutch for 'John,' who applied it to the English intruders in New York, or rather, New Amsterdam. The English in this case were the Johnny-come-latelies. Ironic that 'John' became slang for 'lavatory,' but that's coincidental, I'm sure.

However, we're digressing even further. Back to the R.P. Guide. *Via* (not *veea*) applies properly only to routes, not methods, so we say, we arrived via Heathrow, but not, via British Airways, especially as you're as likely to end up in limbo.

y

Don't know in exact figures what you can expect, but I can guarantee, with a little tweak here, judicious yank there, we can soon pull your finances into shape. How old are you now, did you say?

There you are. At your age, I had nothing. Nothing. Now look at me. All achieved by shrewd investment. A few people thought I got lucky, but no, luck doesn't enter into it. You have to take a few risks, naturally, but you cover the risks. That's the secret, cover your risks.

Spread-betting? No, that analogy with horse racing is one I never make. Bloodstock and Stock Market, entirely different animals. If you'd rather invest in Newmarket, don't come to me, is what I tell my clients. Best way to insult a financial adviser, call him a tipster, or pundit, even worse. Wouldn't upset me, I'm thick-skinned, but then I can afford to be. No, it's not gambling, it's utilising the multiple intelligence of the market. Now, let's get down to brass tacks. Metaphorically, at the moment. This isn't the right time to get into the Minerals field, risks are too great in some areas, rewards too low in others. No, I've taken the liberty of drawing up a list of stocks I think would make a modest portfolio for your financial situation, some long-term rewards, but a degree of liquidity built-in.

No, safe as houses. I've compiled the whole package on the principle of risks and balances, as I said before. Just look at these graphs of the good old Footsie. A few market corrections, blips on the radar, but otherwise, onward and upward. Long may it …

No reason for it not to.

Well, faint heart never won fair million, but …

No no no, fine, no, if you're naturally conservative. Well, you could certainly do worse than Government Stock, yes. Get into Gilts. By association. Gilt by association. It's an old trade joke

I sometimes use, to restore good humour, cover any... On the subject of governments, we do need to look at your tax situation, see what we can eliminate there. No no, legally, of course. But to decrease one's outflow is the equivalent of increasing one's inflow. Simple, but often overlooked by the financial innocent, the, tyro, if you prefer. Now, one little tax-saver I'd recommend would be a ZEBRA. Zero-coupon bond. Bears no annual interest, therefore attracts no tax. Buy it at a discount, in lieu, cash it in on maturity. I take it the question of school fees will loom large in a few years? The perfect solution.

Now, I'll leave you to ponder, consult with the distaff side by all means, give me a tinkle, cheque book in hand, and I'll be right over. Oh, reminds me. Wouldn't have a tenner floating around, would you? Add it to my bill? Damn cabbie wouldn't take a cheque, used up all the readies.

z

never in this country, in the wild anyway. I suppose zebra grass grows in Africa, but I could try it, if I can get seeds, protect it with glass, perhaps. Or if it grows tall, put sticks around it and a polythene sheet. But where would I get the seed? Perhaps they grow it in Kew Gardens. I could ask for extra pocket money, go and see, look in the greenhouses. If they do grow it, I can see how tall it gets, even sneak some seed, or ask them, tell them about my project, they might give me some, want to encourage me.

That would be nine types of grass in my bed, nine species. Species? And I'd have to find out the proper name for zebra grass, make a label. Also see if it spreads. I might have to put a box in the ground and plant it in that, stop it spreading among the other grasses, strangle them, even. It depends on the root system. Mr. Roffey says grasses have a fibrous root system, they spread underground, but some faster than others. He says they're colonisers, spreading into the soil wherever they can, even the smallest bits, cracks in the playground. I've seen that. All types of soil. Even sand, there are grasses that grow in sand, on beaches. Mr. Roffey says if all other plants died, there'd still be grass, spreading out over the land, colonising the world. He once quoted someone, Laurence someone, dreaming about the whole earth with nothing but grass, just grass and rain and wind. He seemed to like the idea. But Atkins said that means we wouldn't be here, even you wouldn't. Mr. Roffey said, yes, that's right.

Now I've thought about it, I think I like the idea too, in a way. It sounds very peaceful. Just the noise of the wind ruffling the grass. And when the wind drops, you could hear the roots spreading, cracking the soil, joining up with other grass, zebra grass, quaking grass, oat grass, fescue, spreading everywhere, even the beaches, right up to the sea. Except there wouldn't be anyone to listen. No Mr. Roffey, but no Williamson or De Doncker either, no one to worry about, no me to worry. I think of that, at night. And when I'm watering my grass plot or planting new ones. Think of them pushing and shoving against the boundary boards. And if the roots can't spread under, they can still send seeds off, spread that way. They all make seeds of some sort, in spikelets. That's what makes it a grass, the seed spikes.

Williamson and his brother kept on and on at me about growing grass in my plot. They meant cannabis. I told them it won't grow outdoors. They kept on, calling me nerdhead and prigprick. They just want me to get into trouble with Mr. Roffey. But I'm not doing the project for Mr. Roffey. It's for me, I want to do it.

Anyway, it's not really a grass. I looked it up. It's Cannabis Sativa, it's in the Mulberry family, it's not even related to the grass family. To be a grass, it has to have hollow stems, with sheaths round them, and straight blades. And it has to have its seed in spikelets, with bristles called awns. To be a proper grass it should be awned

a

benches should be awned, or moved to the shade.
  - They're bolted down.

post-meridian

13.00 Blue neon haze along the top of field of vision modifies the sunlight as it reflects, due to the angle of incidence, from rectangular plate glass bisected vertically by chromed steel bars, which in turn are picked up by two chrome table edges distorted by the shadow, chrome chair leg 15° off vertical, a suited leg, an inch of striped blue sock above black kickboard.

Wide-angle: left field, beyond plate glass, pavement, widening to meet the brick pillars, partially shadowed, of a colonnade; right field, wall, approximate height 4' of grey brick, crumbling in places but with new stone coping, behind which a foliage canopy ripples in reflected light.

(<u>SAVE</u>/DELETE)

I've started to lunch out again. I hadn't been doing so for a while. A sandwich over the drawing board seemed more efficient, more focused. In fact, it was a retreat, a protective reflex from a raw wound. The restaurant I used, where I felt at home, and to which I am only now, after a three year absence, able to return, is the one in which I met, and continued to meet, Judith.

It's a branch of Pizza Express, which I liked at the time for its spaciousness, with a high ceiling, pastel plaster and colourful murals, and long wall glassed to the floor, overlooking the Colne as it rills into the Thames. The ceiling height had an unfortunate acoustic effect, magnifying the unavoidable noise of cutlery and conversation decibels above the comfortable, but I quite liked that. The cocoon of noise quelled any attempt at conscious thought, allowed my idling subliminal mind to race. It made conversation difficult but as I ate alone, that didn't matter. Then, for a while it did, then ceased again, for a different reason.

I had secured, that day, my usual table by the glass wall, was half reading the paper, half watching the ripple of the Colne, occasional glint of fish, not noticing the build-up of lunchtime custom to the point where I was asked, hesitantly, if I would share my table. I agreed with a distracted smile, and withdrew to my thoughts, or non-thoughts, and pizza.

I suddenly noticed a kingfisher perched on the rail of a footbridge further downstream. I'd seen it there before, but it's always a heart-stopping sight however often seen. She noticed my sudden alertness – maybe she'd been watching me, I don't know – and half turned to follow my line of sight.

As she did so, the kingfisher launched itself, arrowed past us, a blur of orange and blue, and swerved under the road bridge. No one else had taken any notice of it, maybe not even seen it. It was a secret between the two of us, like the fall of Icarus in the Bruegel painting. It created an unspoken intimacy between us. Except that she then spoke. With the ambient noise level, I didn't catch it, and automatically apologized.

She said, I'm sorry, I was talking to myself, which is very rude in company. I was just quoting to myself 'After the kingfisher's wing has answered, light to light …'

She'd had to lean forward to make herself heard, and I instinctively did likewise. I recognized the lines, from Burnt Norton. I said, It's not exactly silent though, in here at least.

I remember then being hit by the absurdity, the sheer staginess, of two strangers quoting Eliot over a restaurant table, like characters in Rattigan. Yet it was that very staginess that somehow propelled the situation. Perhaps we were both curious as to how far we could play the scene (I meant to confirm that with her later; never did). So we ad libbed in raised tones that cancelled any undue intimacy, neutralized it into a conversation between friends, or maybe, just fellow guests at a dinner party (I don't actually go to dinner parties, but presumably that's what they are like).

We talked of the view of the Colne, I pointed out the fish, dace, I think, in the stream's boil, told her I'd seen the kingfisher before, and occasional yellow wagtails, who follow the stream down from the moor, where they breed in summer. She was knowledgeable enough about birds to be impressed by the rarity of yellow wagtails in outer London, though it transpired her interest was more literary than field; she preferred Bewick to actual feathers. But her interest was genuine nonetheless, and her knowledge wide, wider than my knowledge of poetry, confined as it was to Eliot, the odd Larkin (the odder the better), and a little Auden, mostly early. She (I should call her Judith, although at that point, I still didn't) was, in contrast, extremely well-versed (again, I learnt that later).

I finished my meal and rose to go, saying I had to get back to my office. She asked, out of politeness, I assumed, what I did. The noise having grown by several decibels, I handed her my card, shouted, If you ever need an extension, and mouthed a goodbye.

She phoned me later the same afternoon. She said, Would you build me a bird hide? I assumed she was joking, and at the time she probably was, but I played along with it and asked when I could survey the site. She said, No time like the present. Come over now.

I did.

The garden was not large, but had an area sectioned off at the bottom, originally as a kitchen garden but now overgrown. What she wanted was a summer house where she could read in seclusion from the house itself. I had already hit on the idea of basing the 'hide' on an actual bird's nest in construction, as a subtle dig at her hands-off approach. But it was more than a joke. I was by then becoming increasingly interested in Green architecture, in both design and materials, so this would have been an interesting exercise even if she weren't serious.

Having now seen the site, I decided to use two existing birch trees, grafting a circular domed construction on to the trunks using a light willow lattice and wire mesh roof overlaid with plaster mixed with horsehair, fibre and feathers, covered inside and out with straw. Modelled roughly on the nest of the marsh-warbler, upturned with a circular step-over opening and disguised skylight, it would be strong, light, warm and unobtrusive, if it could be made to work.

I took the drawings round to her a week later. She was enchanted. We walked down to the bottom of the garden, stood on the spot looking up into the birch trees. Then she said, How much should I expect to give for the erection?

I looked at her. She burst out laughing, saying, Your face, leaned over and kissed me. I knew then she was serious.

My previous failures should have inoculated me, but the virus subtly alters each time, and the immunity anyway wears off.

She was honest with me from the start. Her marriage was by then a sham, a convenience kept going on her part by inertia, helped by her husband's absences - he was an industrial chemist, travelled a lot. She made no promises, and I understood that the force required to overcome her inertia would have to reach critical strength naturally, over time.

I recommended an enthusiastic and reliable contractor, came back periodically to 'check the erection.' Once it was finished and photographed, we agreed we should meet only elsewhere. My place weekends, when she could, the restaurant for lunch. I was playing it by ear, waiting to reach that critical point.

In the event, a stronger force intervened.

In the meantime, we were happy.

In Bertram's in London I found a copy of the paper-covered edition of Burnt Norton, published to complete the individual Quartets, though it was not a First, only a 3rd. Impression. I gave it to her over lunch. We half-expected the kingfisher to materialize, but that only happens in novels.

Over the next two years I managed to track down first editions of each of the Four Quartets, including, eventually, one of Burnt Norton to replace the 3rd.

She in turn sent to America for a rare copy of Frank Lloyd Wright's 'A Testament.'

Our relationship wasn't as high-minded as this suggests; far from it. It was easy, spontaneous, trivially absorbing.

We walked over Staines Moor or Windsor Great Park, sharing my binoculars until she nearly strangled me in her eagerness to spot a skylark and I bought her a pair of her own. Often we just walked. We made love, companionably and chattily, or intensely and silently, but in either case, with an ease that, as Eliot put it, was cause of wonder.

And of course I did wonder. But relationships too are subject to the Uncertainty Principle. As soon as you attempt to observe or probe, you disturb it, alter the dynamics. I resolved to just enjoy it, time by time, leave the future to arrive when it would.

What happened was that on one of his trips, to Canada as it happened, her husband had a slight mishap at a cocktail reception - just a spilt drink and spot of embarrassment, no more. But later, in the laboratory, a similar mishap with a chemical injection which, though not dangerous, was expensive, and serious. When he got home, he had an annual check-up for his company's insurance, and mentioned the incidents. His doctor recommended a precautionary scan. Within weeks it was diagnosed as Huntington's Chorea.

Judith was devastated. Sat in her summer hide all night, trying to come to terms with it.

If she were going to leave him, she'd have to be prompt. But we both knew, without any discussion, it was already too late. We had a tacit agreement that we couldn't be happy at others' expense. The prognosis was uncertain, as regards a timetable. It could be months or years before he needed full care.

We met when we could, enjoyed each encounter, but consoled, on my part at least, with a dimly eventual possibility of being together.

Then her son was knocked down in a hit-and-run, paralysed in both legs, though with a possible full recovery; he, anyway, is optimistic. But for Judith, I suspect it was like the two hammer blows in Mahler's Sixth symphony, that leave you waiting anxiously for a third.

I've only seen her since by chance. But she has never really left me. I wake at night, imagine her there, asleep in my lap against concrete wave upon wave an almost indiscernible movement the water level rising falling by laws of displacement the weight displaced by bodies moving in tandem effortless lap and turn and lap each in turn leapfrogging without winner or loser a displaced world refracted to a viscid darkness rich and strange but a faint breeze adding a surface disturbance hardly measurable on the Beaufort but just discernible in water plucking the bow the algal blooms in riven concrete exposed to brittle sun as the trough drops measurably swallow by swallow in the heifer's slow lap, my arm under hers, hand on her breast, and the faint possibility of still being together in some future life. It couldn't be the same, of course. It could only be contingent on a development that, inevitable though it is, would still colour everything else. And I'm not sure what colour it would be.

This is taking on the nature of a confession. Yet what I'm confessing, to myself at least, is the confusion of feeling. Maybe the only pure emotions are the negative ones: anger, revenge, jealousy, hate. The positive ones are amalgams, in shifting admixture. Bitterness, desire, compassion, a trace of hope. But I wouldn't have missed it, whatever the price.

So, sitting in the pizza house, watching the rill of the Colne, I sense her across the table, her ankle against mine, also drawn by the water's sparkle.

The restaurant has, ironically, been redecorated, with a suspended ceiling and wood panelling, to reduce the noise. We would be able to converse now, without raising our voices or leaning closer. But perhaps, in these conditions, that initial conversation would have petered out in conventional platitudes.

Today, like a blessing, I had a sudden glimpse of a yellow wagtail.

14.00 Unbroken expanse of blue, cerulean, shading to Prussian.
Wide-angle: More of the same. At lower edge of vision, rising from left at
angle of 35°, a flat edge of brick, terracotta the top course, vertically laid,
yellow ochre below in English bond. Toward extreme left a tuft of grass
above the brick.

(SAVE/<u>DELETE</u>)

I should have gone back to the office, started work on the
ventilation modelling of the morning's project, but somehow felt
not ready to face a computer screen. Maybe it was the possibility
of the project now being theoretical, though still worth while as
an exercise. Maybe it was the wagtail. I think it was the wagtail.

But then, an amble over the moor would have been a more
appropriate response. Memory-induced melancholia? But I
didn't feel sad, or not exactly so. You perhaps understand better
than I the mixture of possible impulses. One of them at least,
I later recognized, was a need for self-assurance, self-assertion,
that is, assertion to myself of my sense of being.

For I decided, on a whim it seemed at the time, to revisit a
completed project, one I am quite proud of, though the pride
would in this case be offset by the building's nature.

I intended at first to walk - it's a little way out of town - but
with the heat, and the after-effects of the cocktail in the park
despite the meal and two espressos, I decided to take the bus. It
was quicker than going back to the office for my car. Besides, I
prefer public transport, not just for ecological reasons. It's in part
a matter of practicality – quicker by train in the commuter hours,
so I garage my car in the office lock-up, use it for sites otherwise
inaccessible.

It's also more interesting. I like the egalitarianism of the
omnibus. Architects, more than most, need to be regularly in
touch with communal opinion, the view from the street. There's

a sort of osmotic process, which seems heightened in shared motion.

And it's more fun. You never know who you'll meet, what you'll encounter. As it happens, I met my practice partner that way, though not on a bus – the Tube.

I'd been to see Max Gordon's newly-completed Saatchi conversion. I left well before the rush hour. In fact, the compartment was half empty, and most of the passengers were tourists, which always makes me feel at ease. Nonetheless I sat down opposite a man who evidently wasn't a tourist, yet could well have been. He had a Moleskine notebook on his crossed knee, and seemed to be sketching rather than writing. I could only make out the recto as he turned the page – it was a graphpaper book. But what really gave him away was his pen. It was a Mont Blanc Meisterstück.

I leaned across and said, Are you an architect? He looked startled. He said, How did you guess? I said, The bow tie and glasses. He looked even more startled. He said, I'm not wearing either. I said, Sorry, thought you were. Then smiled. I said, The cigar. The penny dropped, and he self-consciously put the pen in his inside pocket. Then he grinned.

He'd been to a site in Willesden Green, of a rather awkward shape, was jotting down a rough plan and front elevation. We spent the rest of the journey to Waterloo discussing Gordon, John Pawson, Minimalism in general, then, by way of bow ties, Le Corbusier, and in particular the Surrealist details – motorized hedges, grass carpet, outside fireplace – of his otherwise Purist Beistegui apartment in Paris. (I could never bring myself to refer to Le Corbusier as 'Corb' even though it was almost a fraternity thing at architectural college. Neither, I was pleased to notice, did Richard. We both referred to him as Jeanneret.)

We exchanged cards, then, over the next week, phone calls, of sometimes hours at a time, often argumentative, always stimulating.

I was working in a small practice at the time – just two partners, me, drawing and design teams. There had been carefully dropped hints over the previous months of the offer of a junior partnership. It made me uneasy. I couldn't adequately explain why, to myself I mean. I felt valued, work was coming my way which challenged me. Yet I was vaguely apprehensive at the idea of commitment.

I only put my finger on it later. The younger partner had changed his after-shave. His new one gave me a headache.

In the meantime I had invited Richard over for a day out in Egham – cheaper than a trip to France and just as interesting.

I wanted to show him Holloway College, on Egham Hill, now part of the University of London, with added campus buildings in drab neo-modernism, but originally a women's college, built on pills - Holloway's Little Liver Pills – on which the fortune was based. It was part of my childhood. I'd had an aunt who worked in the sewing room, and used to visit her there. Those visits also contributed to my love of bricks, the deep red brick of the walls, with lavish cream stone dressing. I rebuilt parts of it with my terracotta brick set. Only later did I learn of its provenance.

It was built by W. H. Crossland, a pupil of Sir George Gilbert Scott, whose built works, with one other exception, are all in Yorkshire. The college, now seen as one of the peaks of Late Victorian, was inspired by one of the Loire chateaux – Chambord – which Crossland visited several times to sketch the details.

My admiration, and personal connections, had made me somewhat proprietorial toward it; I was worried about Richard's reaction, the weather, seeing it at its best. I needn't have worried. The sun broke through as we arrived, bathed the brick in August light, flashed off the dressing, and we walked the deserted courtyards, as I did in my youth, admired the gatetowers and pavilions, tourelles and cupolas, and, inside, the polygonal vestibule of the Hall.

We had to leave by lunchtime as the college was hired out

for a wedding reception. I suggested we went on to Crossland's other work outside Yorkshire, the sanatorium in nearby Virginia Water, also for Thomas Holloway, whose wife, I understand, had at some time needed psychiatric nursing.

It's less ornate than the College, but quite as interesting, though the influence this time was Flemish: crow-stepped gables, an incredible 19 bays each side of the central hall, and a particularly large hammerbeam roof in the richly ornamented interior.

Which, sadly, we were unable to see. It had recently closed as a sanatorium; was locked and empty. I'd heard permission was being sought to convert it into luxury apartments. If granted, would it be put out in open competition? We discussed the possibilities in purely theoretical terms at first, but with a mounting degree of excitement. For even if this would be tendered by invitation only, there may be other opportunities, with greater freedom for cross-fertilisation between past and present.

And this, it seemed to us, was the right way round; to update the texture of the past, rather than graft traditionalist features onto modernist forms. Or have them grafted on later by traditionalist inhabitants. Which brought the conversation back to Jeanneret – 'Corb' – and his workers' houses in Pessac, whose residents immediately added on all the old-fashioned ornament he had carefully stripped out: pitched roofs, archways, inglenooks. Richard again mentioned - it had become an in-joke between us – his Beistegui apartment, with outside **ingle *(1592)* *a catamite. verb (1595) to fondle, caress.* So an inglenook, he wonders, could that be now a corner of a pub, a bar itself, gay bars he thinks of, writes it in his notebook, turns the pages, a long way to go and he's glad it's only the Shorter Oxford he bought, he's still only a third of the way, but he's on to L now. *Leman from LIEF (dear) + MAN a dear man, an unlawful lover.* There's a lake called that in France or maybe Switzerland he remembers, Lake Leman, could that be code, it seems far-fetched but he's taking no risks, he jots that down, carries on. *Lime (v.) 2 (1555) To impregnate,*** *hence copulate with.* It doesn't seem specific but nothing now is innocent, so he writes down *Limehouse*, ('be prepared'), peruses on into M but that reminds him with a little jolt of the must, the temperature surely must be right by now, get the thermometer out (he smiles at this) he must check the must be an easier way to make a living, average of one gag for every five fags, maybe those nicotine patches would be better, but on second thoughts, it's not just the rush, it's the ritual, enforced distraction of lighting up, that lets the jokes come, dropping your guard, so to speak. Anyway that's my excuse. Maybe something there. *Tried one of those nicotine patches last week. No good. Couldn't move my lips. It's always the unexpected dangers that do you in. Same with drink. Mate of mine nearly died of drink. Whisky. Not cirrhosis of the liver. Acute blood loss. Lacerated his tongue. Well, he'd dropped the bottle.* I can't keep this up. I'm losing *my* bottle, losing my rhythm. I don't have the ebb and flow. Only ebb. *My health's improving, I think. I used to be a manic-depressive. Now I'm... just a depressive.* No. Go back to the office. Ferguson'll have me back. I was good. Good for morale, he said. Good for my morale, at least. Humour comes from context. Not piss-taking. Give and take. None of the fucking hostility I get now. What do I really *They say, make a girl laugh, she'll fall into bed with you. All mine laughed so much they fell straight out the other side.* No, it's not that. It's not being liked I want. Just acceptance. Same at school. In with the cool group. An equal. Security, maybe? That's not it. More a cause, having a cause. Being one of a team, one of the band on my finger, Rupert, that's all it would have taken. A plain gold band is worth any amount of gemstones. But a girl has to play the field until she knows which horse will come home. And you never came home, did you, Rupert? Never came home to me, just dropped in as and when. When you pick up on this, please, don't wipe it, even if you don't call me back, at least don't wipe this. Because I'm pleading, darling, and I can't do it again, I haven't the practice. Just come back to stay, ring or no ring. I'll go on wearing your brooch ironically. Better yet, exchange it. Exchange it for Fire opals, stay, set my life alight two stops before and walk the rest. I like ideally to come upon my buildings by surprise, see them afresh, as a stranger would. It rarely happens, having worked on them for months, years sometimes, designing, drawing, supervising the planning application, construction ... But just occasionally, approach from an unusual angle or direction will give me that glimpse, unfettered from the effort expended, which is the only satisfaction an architect, any artist, can have from his work.

It didn't occur today. Nonetheless, I still enjoyed the accomplishment of the echoes I'd striven for – the grave mounds echoed by the building, echoed in turn by the bank of the reservoir across the A30. I like such echoes, rhymes as it were, a little of the Japanese idea of 'borrowed scenery,' I like to think.

Officially it's finished, already in use (it was used today, by the look of things) but I still have a key, to fuss over a few details I said weren't exact, like the flagstones over the heating ducts from the solar storage, which were several millimetres out of true. Really though, I like to come here to think, or just sit. This is a good place for meditation, especially the more melancholy sort.

Which is as it should be, for that is its purpose. A chapel of rest is for the contemplation of the living, after all, or *by* the living.

It was criticised in its design stages, and subsequently, as being too gloomy, morbid even, for resembling being *in* a grave, which was part of my intention. Contemplative of life and death, certainly, but sitting in it now, sunlight flooding through the solar glass roof, refracting on the flagstones and burnishing the wood panelling walls, I don't find it morbid.

Like being in a coffin with the lid off, someone said, and so it was meant. For the lid *is* off, and later we walk out, through the glazed sliding front, into air and life.

It successfully, I think, overcame the problems. Of site, for one – this is Green Belt land, it couldn't be obtrusive. Ideally, it would have been underground and disguised by earth berms, but there was the carrying of the coffins to consider, a lift system would have been too expensive, even inappropriate perhaps. So I settled for a shallow decline, keeping the building low, three solid walls, wood-panelled within, earth mounded to the roof outside and turfed. Fully glazed roof and front wall, recessed, and a continuation of the rose bed down the middle of the chapel, so running under the lychbench. It's cool in summer (the roof is louvred), warm in winter, quiet – hardly a sound from the planes and traffic. In fact it proved even more practical than I anticipated once they started digging the surrounding field for gravel. And it thus acquired yet another echo – from the now-grassed bunds of the quarry's topsoil, to the side.

Sitting there this afternoon, then, I felt that quiet sense of accomplishment I seem to need more and more in my life. I felt comfortable physically too, I'm pleased to say. The benches I'd specified, in mahogany to match the panelling, and with sculpted backs and seats, are ergonomically succesful, restful but with sufficient mortification of the flesh for the context.

I sat for a while, deep in thought, or rather, deep in nonthought. Then a parakeet's cry scratched into the just-perceptible rumble of the gravel works. It somehow darkened my mood. I needed anyway to justify my visit by checking that the flagstones had been correctly relaid.

They had. But something glittered between two of them. I knelt to look. A needle of some sort. I carefully prised it out with a nail file. It was a hypodermic needle. There was a patch of ground glass on the edge of the flagstone, some larger fragments in the mulch of the rose bed. Someone had obviously scraped aside the broken syringe with their foot.

I felt unaccountably depressed. I tried to imagine somebody – I assume a diabetic – sitting here in view of the coffin, listening maybe to the commonplace eulogy, suddenly being reminded so sharply of their own fragility. It's one thing to philosophise in the abstract, even on one's own mortality, providing it's still vaguely distant, quite another in the concrete.

I buried the needle, pushed it deep into the soil beneath the thorniest rose I could find. But it kept pricking me, pricking my conscience. I thought back to the alcoholic in the park. 'There but for the grace of God …' is an old enough truism, but the point about a truism, as Bernard Levin pointed out, is that it is true. Enough to make me think, at least.

What is it that people – all people, not just diabetics, alcoholics, the problematically challenged – need at times in their life? What I needed today: somewhere to think. There are, I'm aware, an abundance of places for help, guidance, counselling. What people need is a place of self-guidance, of non-counselling. That after all is why I have hung on to the key of this place. But I can't keep it forever. What, then, about building another chapel, not of rest but recuperation?

If I could find a site, I thought, put it to some of my previous clients, contribute the design? But with the most unprepossessing sites the price they are, even a dereliction would be difficult to finance. A short-term lease, the way charity shops, 'pound' shops, operate? I envisaged something longer-termed, and away from the high street. But on the same principle.

Suddenly I had it.

Where better than close to the cemetery? On open land, a short walk out of town? On medium-term temporary lease? Where better than the gravel pit? Once worked, filled in and relevelled it can't be used for building in the foreseeable future. It could only be landscaped for public amenities, as others have been locally, or revert to crops. But there's an awkwardly shaped wedge that was always left uncropped, permanently fallow.

This is also Green Belt, of course. So much the better. What I have in mind is a larger version of Judith's bird-hide. It could even be a bird-hide, in part. The area is surprisingly rich for an urban area. I brought my binoculars when we were surveying the chapel site. A kestrel, skylarks, green woodpecker, jays. In winter, I was told, lapwing, golden plover, fieldfare, teal.

I envisage, then, something on the lines of a Japanese tea house, a structure that would lightly grace the earth, with a built-in fragility. A light hardwood frame and floor, wattle-and-daub exterior (plenty of local clay onsite) using latticed hazel (again, local – old coppices grow around the margin) inner walls of the same, undaubed, with an insulation infill, straw perhaps. Sliding paper screens or blinds to create individual cells, on which, too, could be projected dioramas – a 'virtual museum' of contemporary optimism. All a little idealistic, maybe, but it's idealism we most need today. It would, though, need a caretaker, or – extending the Japanese tea house analogy – a sort of resident *sage and marjoram, served with puy lentils and spinach 7/10. Marinated tuna steak on garlic crouton with fennel and French beans 8/10. Minted lamb and rosemary kebabs with roast peppers and onion 6/10* (too small portions). *Vegetarian Platter with grilled Quorn,* Beaufort and Mid-surrey, concentrate on those three, but Justine, this time, no sabotage. We follow on trail bikes with placards, get the Press onside. I really think the Government are going to pull their finger out this time. We can't risk violence giving them the excuse to bottle out. We'll try to hire a camera, in case the Press bottle out too, follow at a safe distance, then close in at the kill, capture the gore that pierced His side pierces us, but some are insensible. There are those, I have read of them, who are born with no sensation of pain, no warning signs of scorch or cut, a dangerous condition, but to themselves alone. But of those morally insensitive, those seared in their conscience with a branding iron, in the words of St. Paul, are they not in equal danger, mortal danger, to themselves? Are they too not to be pitied? But then, others besides themselves are involved. Is it really a moral equivalent? This is my sticking point. How much I would love to accept the branch. But I fear for the easiness of the acceptance. Am I clear to you on this? And which was it, by the way, widow or mother? Well it makes no difference. So what action now do you expect of me? I'll do nothing that would defile down a valley and over a bridge, I think near Alençon, *oui?* and my father and another covered the rear in a machine gun nest until they were all safely across. *Brave? Oui,* I suppose he was. *Mais non,* not then. No, came unscathed through all that fierce fighting. Wasn't that funny? Well, I suppose they were well hidden in the grass and weeds, and veiled, both of them, walking arm in arm, tightly gripped, picking their way precariously between the graves, as if inebriated, at first sight, but I don't think it was drink. More an excess of emotion. No one else in sight. They seemed alone, so very alone, and forlorn, lost, even to each other. I felt intrusive even by my presence, although they were still a long way off and gave no sign of having noticed me. Nevertheless I decided to make myself scarce. As much to avoid the emotion myself as for their sake. I put my notebook back into my pocket and walked purposefully back toward the chapel, skirting the graves, keeping to the perimeter.

The encounter had rather dampened my creative elation. For how could any chapel, whether of meditation or recuperation, avail such extremes of distress, what dioramas could ameliorate such despair?

But then, I thought, it *was* an extreme, even *the* extreme, and not necessarily the experience of all. There's a spectrum involved. The median also need consideration. Help at least those who can be helped, is a valid rule of thumb.

I decided when I reached the road to walk back rather than wait for a bus. I hoped the exercise would restore my mood. I rather gingerly crossed the A30 and walked along the footpath at the base of the reservoir bank. Further back, there's a pathway up to the top, and a walkway across the middle of the reservoir. It's an excellent spot for birding in winter, especially when they drain the basin for maintenance. I've seen avocets there, tiptoeing through the silt, despite being under the flight paths of Heathrow. I made a mental note to come out here weekend. Even in summer it's worth the trek. I think I caught a glimpse of a juvenile cormorant today.

But that wasn't the only spotting I made. As I rounded the curve of the bank's edge I saw some contraption on the grass verge ahead, behind the perimeter fence. I walked on, in detour, for a closer look.

A house on wheels; not so much a caravan as an old-fashioned bathing hut: iron wheels, well rusted (it appears to be in permanent situ), timber board walls, corrugated iron roof, also somewhat rusted. Yet it appears to be inhabited, or at least in use.

I took out my notebook and sketched it quickly. I collect such 'found' buildings as I travel. There's an old pumping house on another reservoir nearby, derelict but intact, a sturdy functionalist building with the graceful integrity of Victorian public works. The oddest of my collection is a pigsty I saw in Stroud; cement over breezeblock, but ornate, like a Rococo folly. Literally rococo

- it had pebbles and seashells embedded in the cement of the facade.

It's not just buildings I collect, but details, oddities of all kinds. I surveyed a building in Richmond once. In the basement was a staircase that led to the ceiling, like something in a Magritte painting. It transpired that it had originally been a furniture store, the basement later floored over.

There's a loose group of architects in Japan, called The Roadside Observation Society, who also make detailed reports of such oddities. I believe they publish their findings. Mine are for my own amusement. And sometimes, inspiration.

15.00 Downward sloping ramp of rainstained concrete half-lit by dim flourescent stutter, handrail of grey pipe against smudged-graffitied wall. At angle of wall and ramp, a perforated steel gully lengthening into the penumbra.
Wide-angle: Grey meshed wire in grey tubular frame at left; grey tubular frame extending to right, patch of grass, sooted shrubs above kerb of roundabout, between blur of red single-decker bus and partially restored Ford Anglia; extreme right, a dazzle of blue.

<u>(SAVE</u>/DELETE)

I felt in rather better mood again by then, and walked fairly briskly back into town despite the heat (there was still some breeze coming off the reservoir). I felt so good, in fact, that I decided to absent myself a little longer from the office, play truant.

A pint of beer in an old pub seemed a good idea. Then I realized there are no old pubs in Staines now. No old anything much, despite being a town important for its bridges since Roman times. The few historic pubs left in the town centre have all been made over, relentlessly modernised.

On the other hand, the new bars and bistros have a European air to them, especially in the pedestrianised high street and in

European weather. I rather like that. A lager, a coffee, at an outside table – the height of sophistication twenty years ago.

I strolled across the new brick *pavé* toward the awnings of a bistro, and found myself sprawled on the brick, a sharp pain in my head and simultaneously my ankle. A woman was bending over me, one hand shading her eyes, the other on the grip of a pushchair, one of those heavy, three-wheeled off-road types. She said, Are you alright?

I sat up, leaning on one hand. I said, I think so.

She said, You should watch where you're bloody going.

As she walked off, the baby – child, rather, since he must have been at least three – leaned out and gave me the finger. I sat for a moment, noticed a splash of blood on the *pavé* and touched my head. I'd collided, as I fell, with a sculpture - two men carrying a roll of lino (Staines was once, even in my lifetime, world capital of linoleum production).

I stood up a little shakily, dusting my jacket with one hand, dabbing my forehead with the other. I entered the bistro, making straight for the washroom, where I rinsed my handkerchief and waited for the bleeding to stop. Then I limped to the bar.

A girl came across from the till in the shadow, a look of sudden concern on her face. She said, What is happened?

I just couldn't admit to being run over by a pushchair. I said, Nothing, just a touch of the heat. She disappeared back into the shadow, reappeared with a jug of ice and a bar towel. She put the towel over the jug, upended it, and gathered and twisted the corners of the towel. She said, For your head. You wish another for your leg?

I said, No, no, I'll just … alternate, till they melt. You're very kind.

From her accent and her name badge, I thought she was Czech, and was tempted to order a Pilsner as an excuse for conversation, but with my head still oozing blood and my ankle throbbing, I didn't feel up to it. I asked for the wine list, and found a table in the far corner, equally shadowed, where I could bury my head in the ice.

I did talk to her after all when she came over, her sympathetic warmth giving me no option. As it turned out, her name, Marta, is Polish, and I really couldn't face any more vodka, so it turned out for the best. I ordered a half-bottle of **Hock Cart *engraving, school of Palmer, c. 1880, p.o.a.* in deliberate shadow, trestled at 90° to the window, so she has to make a peak of her palm to see through the glass, but she's instantly enraptured, drawn into the scene and back to childhood, the childhood of mankind, all calculation of budget suspended, held by the forcefield of burred striation as sheaf-heaped cart, driver - smocked and hatted - and horse sink down the worked density of rounded hedgerows towards a distant farm, drawn by the white of the setting sun, its horizontal light falling over etched stubble, ageless children on a gate, a single rick**, I think I can walk alright. She said, You are sure? If unsure, I can help you to your office. Look, bar is quiet.

I said, No, I wouldn't dream of imposing. You're very kind. What I will do is drop in for a drink tomorrow, let you see I'm on the mend.

She said, Make sure and do.

I went out with a spring in my step, despite the limp. There was a wagtail under the tables, bobbing about for crumbs. Pied, not yellow, but all the same. And my ankle started throbbing.

And my sock was torn. I hobbled into the department store opposite to buy a new pair, change at the office.

I settled, finally, on horizontal stripes in blue, grey and purple (I'd seen Richard Rogers in a similar pair) and felt quite jaunty as I came out. So much so that, seeing a Big Issue salesman over by the statue, near my drop of blood, I approached him first. I had no change so I gave him a tenner, told him to keep the rest.

He refused. I said, Look, have a drink on me, you must be hot. He pointed out the caption on the cover – Street Trade, Not Street Aid – and insisted on giving me my change in full, and in 50 pence pieces. He seemed too offended to argue with.

I pocketed the coins. In several pockets, actually. Then walked slowly back toward the office.

It made me think, though. The whole issue of housing need, and especially what I term Beneficiary housing.

One of the reasons for my pride in my profession is that advances are often made precisely because of such social concern. The Garden City, for example, workers' housing, Bournville, Port Sunlight. Or Le Corbusier's 'Dom-ino' system of prefabricated concrete houses, driven by the acute need for replacing the houses destroyed by the outbreak of the First War, in Flanders particularly.

Similarly here in Britain during and after the Second. A lot of experimentation went on on the prefabrication idea, both in designs and materials - rock wool, sawdust concrete for infills, aluminium from aircraft scrap and from the post-war production capacity of the aluminium and steel industry in the switch from war material after 1945.

I went once to the Buildings Museum in Bromsgrove, where they have a Mark V Arcon prefab. house preserved. Odd at first, but beautifully and painstakingly designed. A curved crown on the roof rather than a pointed ridge, for strength, in place of steel jointing at the apex. Single-skin cement for the roof, double-skin for the walls with glass-fibre insulation. Care, too, in the details - steel architraves, skirting boards that doubled as ducting for the electrical wiring. Fitted fridge and cupboards, drop-down table, hot-air ducts from the boiler to the bedrooms, although these, according to residents, weren't entirely effective.

Only around 40,000 were eventually built. And of the dozen or so brands in the Temporary Housing Programme, a total of around 150,000, a small proportion of the houses needed. What's interesting, though, is the durability of the structures, which were only designed for a life of 15 to 20 years. It's true they developed, early on, problems with insulation, condensation and so on. But also the degree of fierce loyalty they inspired in their residents, despite those problems, some living in them until the turn of this century, refusing offers of rehousing, obstructing local authority plans to demolish them.

Originally, I assumed, it was the community spirit of the immediate post-war that inspired this loyalty, the excitement of getting a home of one's own, the advances in modern facilities. But that would have worn off eventually. I now think the loyalty derived, at least in part, from the sense of involvement they felt. Largely illusory, maybe, since one of the points was the standardisation of all the parts. But they were involved, first by the Government at the initial experimentation stage, invited to comment on prototypes, for example the one erected outside the Tate Gallery. And later, involved, or felt themselves to be, in the erection process - which was typically a single eight hour day - either watching or even helping.

And I suddenly linked that to the Big Issue chap. People want to be involved, to help themselves. There is almost as acute a need for housing now as then. Not for what architects generally mean by 'affordable housing', which usually means affordable by bank managers, but genuinely affordable. Self-build, self-help schemes. We need similar experiments in new cheap materials. New designs.

I remember watching my father, in his retirement, endlessly making papier-maché briquettes. They were not for building but fuel. My parents had a pre-war semi-detached with no central heating, just an oven-type coal fire. To save money, he bought a patent brick-maker. You tore newspaper into strips, soaked it in a bucket of water, poured the mash into the mould and pulled a lever that squeezed out the water and compressed the paper into a brick, which was left to dry, then burnt, which it did very slowly.

I thought, suppose the same process were used for building bricks? Bricks from pulped surplus Big Issues, perhaps? Or newspaper generally. I'm quite serious about this. Self-build from scratch. Like sawdust concrete, some additive to the mix to make it waterproof, or a coating after the wall is built, in double thickness with insulation.

New structural designs would be needed. Or very old ones. The igloo, for example. Or the beehive cells of Kerry. The oddest example of the Prefabrication ideas from abroad that were under consideration after the war was the American Bubble House, built by pouring concrete over an inflated canvas balloon, forming, in shape, precisely an igloo. I don't think it was tried here, but apparently was in use in the States.

We are talking genuinely temporary here. But better than a cardboard box, more private than a hostel. A breathing space. The idea could be developed, used abroad. There's a great deal of verve and inventiveness in the shanty towns of the world. The ultimate self-build. And sadly, shanty towns are here to stay, here to grow.

I wanted to bounce the ideas off Richard straight away, but I felt they needed to simmer, percolate for a while. Later I wondered if the ideas weren't the effect of the sun, wine and fall, but I still feel there's merit in them.

I remember, a few years ago, Millenium Year I believe, a Japanese pavilion for that year's Expo was built from carboard tubes and bamboo, and beautiful it was too. Admittedly designed for a very short life and specifically to biodegrade afterward, but the potential was demonstrated, and could be adapted for longer term use, with an outer membrane, for example.

A simple timber frame, moulded-paper brick walls, pitched roof of waterproofed tubular cardboard, the whole thing built from scratch by the homeless themselves, working as teams, with minimal supervision. A suitable site provided by the council, a drop-in one-piece water unit, and electricity supply would be all the outside help they'd need. Even the furniture could be self-made, from moulded cardboard pulp (again, it's been done in Japan). The important thing is the involvement of the beneficiaries, even at the design stage. And a little initiative and vision.

Therein lies the snag.

16.00 Extreme close-up of inverted chrome tap, lever-operated, reflection from lever of marble rim, white ceramic basin, red- and brown-streaked water to within inch of rim.

Wide-angle: Inverted image of marble top broken by three chrome taps, three white basins, top abutting eau-de-nil plaster wall, extreme right; eau-de-nil expanse broken by wood panel, silk-finish vertical steel bar, circular chrome lock, extreme left.

(SAVE/<u>DELETE</u>)

It was a little before four by the time I got back to the office. I took off my glasses, bathed my head and ankle, changed my socks.

Linda insisted on putting a plaster over my forehead. I noticed she'd had her hair done, presumably in her lunch hour. Does this mean she has a date? She said nothing about it, but she did seem cheerful. Maybe it's just the weather. Fingers crossed.

Richard was still out on site. I decided to get down to checking the drawings for the hospital project so I can send them to the model-makers in time for the deadline. I've done the sketch, the 'artist's impression' already, by hand. I still prefer the old-fashioned way to a computer projection. And the old-fashioned scale model too, though in this case it was one of the criteria of the competition, still beats computer realizations. You get a better sense of the building's presence, its weight and **heft had moved up along the bank, he's searching in his gaze for the stragglers, a purely reflex concern as there's no danger they could get into, his unease comes rather from the inaudible rumble that now sharpens as the plane rises from behind the reservoir. Impossible yet to work out its eventual flight path, destination. But at least a proportion of them head east, to Amsterdam, Warsaw, on to Russia, and in a mathematical sense one of them will one day carry Velta. He puts the thought, but not her, from his mind, is** reminded by her name to go back to the river, check on his keepnet, well enough hidden, he hopes, but you never know with southrons. He walks toward the perimeter gate. Out of luck with the umber but he has struck it with another, a fine sized barbel, a good sixpounder. Handsome too, not a fish he knows from home, and he's surprised because the books all say it's a slow-river fish, a bed-feeder, and he can only think his long-trotting took his line into a pool, a backwater, so maybe the fish was as surprised as he was, put up a fight though, thrashing and plunging, but he's safe in the keepnet. Too hot to kill it and keep it in the hut, and he's not sure if it's worth the eating. They're eaten in Europe but he's not sure where, he wants to ask Velta. No point killing the poor thing for nothing. But at least she'd see it, know it was no fancy-taling. Why, he wonders, do taste buds differ, by place and by time, for not only in Europe but in England gone by, coarse fish were eaten and enjoyed, from the recipes found in Izaak Walton, pope, perch, loach, dace, that wouldn't be looked at now, where others are today counted a delicacy, like tench, Lakeland *char in a fire banked with turves so the birch just smoulders should be him roasting sadistic old faggot what he ever teach me stretch and size his canvases fetch and mix his drinks ghastly sub-Sickert neo-Camden daubings not burning properly blow on it need some bellows could be a scene from Thomas fucking Hardy Woodlanders was it one of the early ones Return of the Native no that wasn't charcoal burning something though a colour ruddy reddy* reddle man *to do with sheep sheep tupping a dye daubed on the ram's chest show which sheep he'd mounted red ochre natural where was it from could use that the who's fucked who of English art why they're all so raddled patches red ochre overlaid by maroon what I am now self-freed one bound and away proverbial eel in an oil* slick post-modern or even neo-modern, adjunct to the existing building - a standard rectilinear white – but something more contextual, both in its surroundings and in its use. I started to think from the view of the patients. Day surgery may not be as frightening as an in-patient operation but it's still an ordeal, even, especially, in the waiting.

I thought too of the locational cues, geographical, historical. I normally like to study a site carefully, even camp out on it if it's a green-field site. But camping on the asphalt of a Tesco car park would have been counter-productive. And in this case, uniquely perhaps, the building will be viewed from above, from the planes in and out of Heathrow.

And, to bring down the cost, financially and environmentally, I wanted to use local resources where possible. Which in this area means gravel.

A few years ago, when the Government replaced a long-demolished borstal with a women's prison, archaeologists unearthed a Bronze Age settlement on the site, a series of post-built roundhouses skirting a Neolithic ringditch.

I decided to use this as the main cue. So, a large circular drum of spaced timber columns, with a double skin, the outer of glass, the inner a permeable membrane, the space between planted with trees, vines, shrubs.

The surgeries in the centre, surrounded by the clerical and reception staff behind a circular counter, leaving the area round the perimeter as a continuous corridor-cum-waiting room, benched all round, with uninterrupted views of the plantation. There is, to me, nothing so calming as living plants when under stress. And on an equally practical level, with natural controlled airflows, they will act to cool and oxygenate the building.

A slightly domed roof with centrally glazed panel to bring immediate daylight to the surgeries, augmented by LED spotlights, the remainder a spiral of membraned guttering overlaid by gravel, to catch and filter rainwater for grey use. Then the whole surrounding area gravelled over the existing asphalt, so from the air the building almost disappears.

I'm thinking of extending the gravel inside, round the

perimeter corridor, with spaced flagstones, to add to the park/ greenhouse effect. If that too were laid over membraned sluicing, it could simply be hosed and raked in the daily cleaning, which would help to humidify the building during the day.

I'm sure it will all cut no ice with the bureaucrats, who will go for the usual uninspired hangar. But we have to try. The public consultation will at least raise the issues.

I have put a lot of thought into this, more than usual, since I may very well be one of its users at some point. Which reminded me that I should have picked up my X-rays from the clinic on the way through town. I decided to ask Linda to do it, save me the stress. A good excuse too to let her leave early, in case of a date, maybe a small bonus to splash out on perfume or shoes or whatever enhances an evening out for women. She might need a hand-written note. For the X-rays.

I don't approve of private medicine, and any treatment I may have would be National Health. It's just that doctors, G.P.s especially, have all signed up to the Hypocritic Oath. There's an unspoken assumption that you're there to be cured, and will take whatever treatment they offer. I just want to know, and know what my odds are. Then I'll decide.

By going for the X-rays privately, it's down to me to inform my G.P., set the machinery in motion.

Of course, if I do need and decide on treatment, it may well not be a Day Surgery procedure. But it's enabled me to empathise more deeply with the patients' needs. I did once have Day Surgery, for a mole on my cheek, which took ten minutes to excise after three hours of waiting, in a windowless room painted magnolia, with geographical analogues in the worn lino for distraction. I just believe we can do better.

I wrote a note of authorisation, put it in a sealed envelope for the clinic, a fifty pound note in another for Linda, and sent her out, telling her to come back tomorrow. Then started checking the elevations.

I was just working on the plan, half an hour later, when, to my dismay, Linda returned. She had, conscientiously, assumed the X-rays were important, insisted, despite what I told her, on bringing them straight back. Which meant her now leaving at her normal time, catching the traffic, arriving home late and flustered.

Well, I tried.

I also felt a little disappointed at the idea that she feels she's at my **beck, or would it be a burn? No, a burn is Scottish, although you once told me there's a technical difference, that strictly speaking a beck has a gravel bed, not like the peat-bedded streams of Scotland, and that a gravel bed meant they flow quicker, that made them better for watermills. You said that's why industrialisation started in the north, on the quick little rivers of the Pennines and the Peaks. You also told me that the Industrial Revolution was powered by water for longer than people realize, long after steam, that sometimes steam engines were used only to pump water to the millraces. Life, as you used to say, is always more complicated than we think. I remember thinking, for example, what about London? That was the biggest industrial city in the country. But then maybe it wasn't so much the Thames, that was more for transport, maybe the factories were powered by all the little rivers that have now been lost, buried and forgotten, not even connected to their street names. The Fleet, Effra, Peck, Stamford Brook, Walbrook and Wandle, Tyburn, Ravensbourne. I always feel so sad at the loss of these London streams, diverted or dried up, or worse, becoming underground sewers.**

I wish I'd said all this to you. Wish even that I'd voiced my doubts over some of your theories. You used to bristle when your word was questioned, but at least you would have known I was listening, was interested, wanted so much to share your enthusiasms. I wish too I'd shown you how pleased I was when you began to share mine, when I got over my fear of being humoured.

Still, if you were with me now we'd have left by now. A quick coffee and cake in the Orangery then you'd have wanted to be off. I'm going back for another coffee and an elderflower *pressé* in a while. I want to get my money's worth, stay until dusk. You'd be complaining by now, wanting to go home and adapt what we've seen to our own garden. That little fence round the bulb meadow, for example, of willow stems twisted round palings. Raddled, I think you once said. You'd want to go home and make one for the scree bed. You always wanted to be active, busy. Never able to just look, contemplate. I worry, how you're coping now with the inactivity. Have you learnt yet to be *still behind the old bandstand, save all this to-ing and fro-ing to the fuckn offy. Make our own vodka.*

- What from?

- Potatoes.

- Potatoes? That's poteen.

- Only if it's Irish potatoes.

- And what?

- What?

- Potatoes and what else? What's the recipe?

- How should I know? We'll look it up in the library.

- Course. Bound to be a book on How To Make Your Own Moonshine in Staines library.

- And how long's it take? How long before we taste it?

- Forever, cause he'll by lying there with his tongue under the drip. We'll no see a drop. Moonbeam more like.

- No, you know me, share and share alike. Still, yeah, making the still might be a problem. We could make the cider though, no problem, real stuff, not this cat-piss. Just need apples, a press and a barrel.

- You know the method, I suppose?

- Course. Watched it many a time. Helped, too, sometime.

- When?

- *When I was a lad. Went applepicking every year for years. Fortnight in Sussex every autumn.*

- *What about school?*

- *Sod school, this was work. Happiest days of your life. Hard, mind. But, when you're young. Nippers gathered the windfalls, older ones picked. Could smell the ferment already in the windfalls. Fresh air, first bonfires. When I got older like, I'd stay on a few days, help with the pressing. You grind up the apples into pulp, put a layer of straw at the bottom of the press, pour in the pulp, more straw, wind the press down, pour the juice into a tub, throw in a lump of meat, Bob's your uncle.*

- *Meat?*

- *Steak or what have you. Mellows the cider. Disappears after a few weeks. Cider feeds on it.*

- *Meat-eating cider?*

- *Cox's Fly Trap.*

- *True's I'm sitting here. Could never wait for the tasting, had to get home, but they'd give me some of the previous year's. Smooth as your mother's milk, lot more kick.*

- *Tha how you became an alkie, then?*

- *No, it was his mother's milk.*

- *Leave my mother out of it. Tried her best. I wanted to stay on in Sussex, they were looking for farmhands. But I was needed at home. Only a fuckn paper round, but it made a difference. Then the window cleaning.*

- *With yer little ukelele.*

- *Look, if you're just going to take the piss, you can go and get the next lot. And a quarter bottle. How's the kitty? Right, get a half, two bottles. Here, take the empties, stick them in the bottle bank on your way.*

- *Pity there's no money back on them these days. Used to be. Tuppence a bottle, old money. Handy little earner.*

- *Bollocks. You paid tuppence extra for the drink in the first place. Money back. You paid a deposit in the price. Now the prices are* net was empty when he pulled it out, he still can't quite work out how. It hadn't seemed disturbed, and when he shook it out, spread it on the ground, there was no sign of a hole in the mesh, couldn't have been a pike, and it's not pike water, but what else, unless emptied deliberately, returned to the water, protester maybe, an anti-*angling for a higher mark, and I feel so grateful, I almost gave it him, but it wouldn't have been professional, would it? Never mind, class is over - my last today - and so too, soon, will term. Then the interminable days.*

The epistolic mode is, for someone such as I, the default mode, to use a modish phrase; I seem to express myself, cogently or ardently, only on paper. Maybe, then, necessity will be a virtue. This is my second letter to you today, and the vacation (how ominously empty that word) has yet to start.

What is the collective term for billets-doux? A bouquet? A flurry? I think, in this case, a blizzard. Prepare for a blizzard of billets-doux, my love.

But tongue-tied warmth is what I most crave. So, I propose a sort of halfway house in our separation. They are doing Mahler in the Proms next month. Could you manage that? I will suggest, for form's sake, that Ginette come with me, but she likes nothing later than Bach, so I feel safe in asking her.

The work is Das Lied. *Do you know it? The words are, by strange coincidence, again by Bethge, again from the Chinese (what is it with Germans and China?). I hope I can sit through it dry eyed. It may alter your conception of me (assuming - presuming - you come. Do I presume too much?) The finale, the Farewell, has always given me trouble. The sinking sun, falling shadows, wind through the pines, and the moon, the moon floating above the blue sea-heaven,* eine silberbarke, *a silver bark* of a dog in a distant flat, *tut* of the clock. He sits with his tea cooling in the mug, a Royal Doulton decorated with a goldfinch, one of a pair. The other, with a chaffinch, is kept for best, unused. In case of visitors. He's transferred his day's tally from notebook to full log, he's up to date on that now. He checks the calendar - a perpetual, aluminium-cased, that you wind on manually - against the date on the newspaper. Once you retire, you revert to the old concepts of time, measuring by the daylight, the seasons, though they can't be trusted now, even the birds get confused, migrating later, nesting earlier. Other than that, it doesn't affect him too much, but all the same, he likes to recalibrate every so often. The silence has seemed longer today. Usually by now it's broken by schoolkids passing the flats. Their noise, chirping, squabbling, like sparrows in a hedge, is welcome, a reassurance, more noticeable by its absence. He's wondering if they've already broken up. He always knew the term dates on his milk round, by the extra pints, snacks, juice. He's out of touch now.

He hears them, turning into the estate, swearing, a football being kicked against the wall of the block. Detention, perhaps. The whole class? He wonders what behaviour would elicit that these days. Their noise gets nearer, approaching in eddies as they stop to argue, move on. It's life. He welcomes it. But not today. Today he decides to close the window, despite the heat, until they pass. He leans out to grasp the catch, glimpses a bird wheeling over the estate. It's a juvenile wood pigeon but just momentarily, he mistakes it for a sparrow hawk but couldn't shift it from my chest, succeeded only in bringing up gall on the trunk of this oak infection insects or something oakgall used to be collected used for ink dyeing wonder what colour colour doesn't matter just a correlative what it symbolizes see if I can slice no pen-knife's no good how did they harvest did it commercially once long time ago aren't enough oaks now dying out chopped down for the navy ended up having to import but it's probably nothing. Even if it is serious I just want to know, have time to acclimatise before I decide on treatment. Death in itself no longer scares me.

Months ago, maybe a year, I woke in the night with a pain in my chest. It grew steadily worse, darting up my throat, into my jaw, then gradually subsided. In retrospect I put it down to the cold cure capsules I'd taken last thing, sticking in my gullet. But at the time I was convinced it was angina, the onset of a heart attack.

What surprised me a little was my reaction. One of overwhelming relief. You may find this morbid, perverse. I had no particular worries, no distrust of life. No more than the general attrition, the untidiness of things, the day to day effort. But the thought of all that being over, the accounts drawn up and closed, nothing more to be done, came as a release of a tension I hadn't even been aware of. It was like the sudden, *given* solution to a design problem after a night's sleep, the unexpected but, in hindsight, prepared for cadence.

The pain passed, and obviously I didn't die. I went back to sleep, woke up feeling fine, carried on with my life. But the experience too lived on, subtly tilted my perspective. The way that out-of-the-body experiences are said to do, though I certainly wouldn't claim it as one of those.

What led me on to this? Yes, the X-rays.

I shooed Linda off for her date, put the envelope in my briefcase, carried on checking the plan. All the drawings are finished, tubed, ready for despatch to the model-maker's tomorrow.

Evening Light

17.00   Horizontally slatted wooden blind, partially open, each slat bearing a strip, foreshortened, of a View of Mt. Fuji. Visible between the slats, grey and mould-green concrete, browning metal frames, glass panels of office block (rear elevation).
Wide-angle: Left of window, egg-blue matt wall, inverted U of aluminium-finish coil loop radiator, far left, at right angle to wall, grey enamel side of filing cabinet. Right of window, expanse of egg-blue, broken by brushed aluminium frame with (left half visible) print of The Academy of Architecture, Berlin, by Karl Friedrich Schinkel, from the painting of Eduard Gärtner.

(<u>SAVE</u>/DELETE)

Richard came back to the office a little after five, looking quite elated. He had been out on site, a conversion job I knew he'd enjoy. We looked over it together when it first came up; a disused school, Late Victorian, a local Board School opened in 1901 and still in use as a Junior School until twenty years ago, when the school merged and moved in with another. The building was then used by a printing firm for a while, partly for its size and space, but when the business failed, it stood empty. There was talk of using it as a local authority adult education arts centre, but the degree of apparent dilapidation put it beyond the council's limited budget. They proposed demolishing it, replacing it with sheltered housing, which would have been a wasteful expense. Despite the deterioration, the fabric is sound. Victorian buildings were, after all, built to **last covered with several layers of tissue paper to protect the vamp, seats the heel. There's a rattle of the door - he's closed early - but he ignores it, absorbed with the feel of kid to his fingers, the leatherscent of newly worn shoes, still supple from** use. However often they're polished, unworn shoes stiffen, dry. As well be in a museum, glass case at least. But the few pairs she left behind have only sentimental value, the choice pairs, the vintage, she took. Gracing carpets now in Aden or Azerbaijan or whichever diplomatic mission her new husband's attached to. There's no rancour left, admiration, if anything. Up sticks, move on - an ability he'd love to acquire. Excitement. But no. Maybe, oddly, that was a bonus. Security was what she sought, beyond whatever he could offer. The fear of well-heeled destitution, reducement. Memories she had confided of her mother, of Ferragamos, Dior gowns, regularly taken in to pawn in local planning politics.

The upshot was that it was acquired by a private client for his own use, and spare apartments.

It's unusual for a Board School in being single-storey - they were generally multi-storey, in crowded urban areas. This, for a smaller roll, in, at the time, a much less urbanized town, was closer to a parish school, but without the teacher's living accommodation.

But it made full use of its single-storey status in the loftiness of its proportions. Light and air were of particular concern to the later reforming Victorians, and there was both in the school, especially in the main assembly hall-cum-schoolroom, with a high ceiling and tall windows extending up into the gables.

It was that, I would guess, that attracted the client; I understand he has an extensive art collection he wishes to show off (though not of course in the Saatchi league).

When Richard and I visited, it was still cluttered and accreted. Now it has been cleared and stripped back, ready for a detailed appraisal. Which is why he'd been out so long. And was now eager to talk.

I suggested we discuss it over a drink. He eyed my plastered forehead, asked if that was wise. I ruefully owned up about how it had happened, how worried the Polish girl had been, suggested we went back there, to set her mind at rest.

We walked back into town.

When we entered the bar, she was nowhere to be seen, presumably off-duty. I suppose I looked a little disappointed.

Richard said did I know her name? I said, Marta.

He said, She ought to be working in Starbucks.

I looked puzzled. He said, Starbuck Marta.

I asked him if he knew the Szymanowski – he doesn't (I must get him a copy). Richard ordered two glasses of Chablis, and we got on to the conversion.

He intends it to be that, a conversion, not a slavish period restoration. Internally, respecting the original proportions, and keeping some salvageable details, for example the wall-mounted blackboards as backdrop to fitted display units, but also working against expectations: using birchwood or ash instead of oak and mahogany; replacing the high wooden skirting with bronze-finish polished steel heating ducts.

Externally he wants to be more conservationist, enhancing rather than altering, adding only for practical reasons. There's a high, now rather unsafe, brick wall round the playground. He intends to demolish it, replace it with salvaged wrought iron, and use the bricks to build on a bell tower, counterbalanced by the existing main chimney, in a ratio (tower to chimney) of 8:5. The tower would not be, he was quick to point out, a mere embellishment (I ignored the pun) but would function as a ventilation stack.

He is, however, thinking of colonnading three sides of the playground, and either tiling or turfing the resulting quadrangle. It was my turn to invoke the Corbusian 'grass carpet'. Richard said, I'll come back to that, told me about the flooring within the school.

Now they have lifted the industrial carpet tiles and layers of lino, the original wooden flooring is exposed, along with a central groove in the main assembly hall/classroom, corresponding to another in the ceiling.

I surmised that there was originally a folding partition sliding between the grooves, to convert the hall into more manageably sized classrooms after morning assembly. I remember my Infants' School had one similar. I also remember it took the janitor and two teachers to slide it into place every day.

Richard wants to restore the idea, as a way of increasing hanging-space in what will be the gallery. I suggested parallel hanging-tracks suspended from the ceiling, enabling the partition to be made of canvas. Not only lighter to manoeuvre, but more adaptable – a way of modifying the light by extending the length, using the concertina pleats in varying overlays.

Richard said he'd consider that, then went back to the exposed flooring. He'd noticed something else set into the floor, which seems distinctly puzzling: a series of brass strips forming a row of inverted Ls in the assembly hall, and continuous parallel strips, like tramlines, the length of the corridors.

The Ls, we guessed, were for the orderly line-up of pupils, class by class, in school assembly. The lines in the corridors reminded me, I said, of the yellow line painted on the ground in the Barbican to stop concert-goers getting lost.

Richard's theory is that they were to direct pupil-flow along the corridors without congestion. There appear to be no markings on the strips, although they might have worn away. But markings wouldn't anyway be needed – a simple injunction to keep the line to their immediate right would ensure an orderly two-way flow.

He said he'd love to know if the strips, in some form, extended into the playground, buried now under generations of asphalt. I said, Surely that would defeat the object of play – the randomness of movement, a space of allowed anarchy between the straits of discipline.

He said, Yes, but re-entering the school at the end of play, there would have to be a switch from chaos to order quite rapidly, especially with several entries into the building. They would presumably have to line up first, march in straight lines.

That's when he brought up – for no good reason I could see – the 'Stuttgart Grass Square'.

I said, Is it related to Corbusier's 'grass carpet'? He said, Yes, by reverse logic.

I have actually heard of it, but I didn't like to spoil his fun. It's related to the realm of urban planning, including that of parks, open spaces as well as the built environment, a topic dear to the hearts of a certain type of architect, Le Corbusier being one of the most prominent examples. Witness his plans for 'A Contemporary City For Three Million Inhabitants' or the 'Plan Voisin', which would have entailed demolishing large swathes of Paris; or his later 'Ville Radieuse'; or the 'Plan Obus for Algiers', which would have necessitated tearing down half the casbah, rehousing the inhabitants in a giant, elongated apartment block with a motorway along the roof.

Admittedly the whole visionary planning mind was a response to the social upheavals of the Industrial Revolution, followed by the first War and Russian Revolutions.

And indeed the Victorians and the Modernists had much in common in their response. Both had rectilinear and rigidly hierarchical models in mind when planning people's lives. The Modernists the more so. At least Victorian architects on the whole contented themselves with streets and buildings. They didn't, with maybe the exception of William Morris, go on to dictate the lives of their clients, designing not just the furniture but cutlery, even the clothes to be worn in the buildings.

There has, naturally, been a move away from this rectilinear, imposed approach to something more organic, especially in the recent application of Complexity Theory to urban planning. And attempts to study how people actually move, behave, when left to themselves.

Which is where the 'Stuttgart Grass Square' comes in, as Richard was eager to expound to me. A few years ago, a group of researchers in Stuttgart University hit on the simple expedient of observing the actual paths people, mainly students, took in crossing the square to the surrounding buildings on the campus, the paths showing up as wear on the grass.

The paths that built up weren't strictly logical – they didn't represent short cuts; the shortest routes would have been straight lines, these were curved, and avoided the centre. It was, rather, a 'fuzzy logic'. Maybe there were slight variations in gradient to account for the initial route, maybe it started spontaneously by someone's erratic path, but having been established, worn even lightly into the grass, they were generally followed, and the wear became more pronounced, and so on.

I said to Richard, There's a simple solution, especially in Germany. 'Keep Off The Grass' signs. He thought I was missing the point. Actually, the signs and the paths work, I believe, in the same way – politeness. If you're going to walk across the grass, why spoil more of it when there's already a bare path?

Planners tend to reduce the logic of crowd movement to two factors: attraction and repulsion; sticking closely with friends, or maintaining their personal body space with strangers. I would reduce it to politeness and panic.

I do in fact agree with Richard on the principle behind all this, the organic, human-oriented approach, based on natural, observed behaviour, in place of the Central Planning ethos. As Karl Popper would say, if something works in theory but not in real life, the theory is wrong because it's there to *explain* real life. Or as even Le Corbusier himself put it, Life is right, the architect is wrong.

Yet I feel a profound need to challenge the whole idea. I wasn't entirely sure why at the time. I did, however, say I rather distrust drawing strong conclusions from such research; the shortest route is still a straight line, after all. And it seems to me we could end up substituting one pseudo-scientific idea for another. I can see dangers in the unscrupulous use of all this. If, for example, computer models could show likely flow-paths within public buildings, someone somewhere will eventually suggest economising on structural support in the lesser-used areas. There are always jerrybuilders in society. How many buildings collapse in earthquake zones through slipshod and corrupt avoidance of building regulations?

It happens here too. Ronan Point was only the most spectacular example. Of the surge of Sixties medium and high-rise blocks, ten thousand had to be demolished within a decade or a little over, due to structural defects. Any pseudo-scientific justification for cutting corners would be welcome even today.

How little, after all, would it take to alter people's directional behaviour. A puddle, a fallen person, and the whole dynamic changes, even without invoking panic.

Thinking back, I was obviously over-reacting, and deliberately misconstruing Richard's argument. In fact, I don't think he had one, just making interested observations. But I think now that the resistance I felt went deeper, to some sort of Romantic belief in the primacy of the individual.

Maybe that's why I've never bothered myself with planning theory, or corporate signature buildings. Such things need addressing, I've no doubt. But it's a little like Quantum Mechanics. One can only deal accurately with matter at the molecular level and beyond. Below that, at the sub-atomic level, the approach has to be probabilistic. The path of a disturbed electron can only be guessed at.

And I tend to identify with that lone, disturbed, electron.

Looking back now, I'm a little worried at the tone - rather, my tone - of the discussion. It was, after all, a purely academic debate by two disinterested, but intensely interested, colleagues. But as I said, my arguments covered an irrational though, to me, entirely valid, premise, and may, for that reason, have become intemperate. I hope not.

In the normal course of events, we would have talked our way through, or talked ourselves out, moved on to other topics and further drinks, and parted leisurely. Unfortunately, the failing of my memory precluded the normal course. I suddenly remembered I had tickets for a concert at the Festival Hall, and was somewhat behind schedule.

To make matters worse, Richard was beginning to tell me, in a roundabout manner, of a commission his client had hinted at, in Qatar. I had the feeling he was sounding me out, in case it solidifies. It's certainly a good one, a new complex for expatriate workers, the chance to design and build from scratch, on virgin sites, and pioneer some new approaches in ecologically-sound structures and cooling systems. It would be good for Richard, good for the partnership. I would have told him so. But in the haste of my departure I made some flippant comment on squares of sand, or worn paths in the desert, I can't recall exactly, and rushed off for my train.

I hope now I didn't give the wrong impression. I'd want him to take it. But miss him if he goes.

18.00 Expanse of coarse-grained mottled green, silver green and silver grey, small patch of light ochre, rougher-grained, left of centre.
Wide-angle: More of same, glimpse of blue, extreme left, grass green, extreme right.

(<u>SAVE</u>/DELETE)

By breaking into a run, then resting against a tree, I just caught my train home. I could have gone straight to Waterloo, with time to spare, but I really wanted a shower and change of clothes. My linen suit was distinctly rumpled – I looked, at least felt, like Frank Gehry. In the event, all I had time for was a shave and clean shirt. Luckily, of course, my socks were fresh.

I hurried back to the station, hoping to be in time for the earlier but slower train, via Hounslow and Brentford. I'm cheered always by the sight of the minaret tower of the Victorian pumping station of Kew Bridge Water Works.

To my dismay, I found the booking office had closed early, and someone was using the automatic ticket machine. Abusing it, in fact. I couldn't see what the problem was, but neither his ticket nor money was forthcoming, and having apparently exhausted all combinations on the touch screen, was resorting to the old pre-I.T. method of banging it. With still no success, he stood on one leg, leaned back quite gracefully, and started to kick the coin slot with his heel, hoping, I assume, to *jar in Tennessee and round it was upon a hill. It made the* something *wilderness surround that hill* but this is hardly wilderness, quite the opposite and it's not a jar more like a Grecian urn in what would it be, you'd know, bronze perhaps but it made me think of that painting we saw in the National Gallery of St. John Entering the Wilderness climbing up the bare rock mountainside and that made me think of you entering your monastic life but you said, you were quite indignant, it's not a monastery it's an entirely secular retreat I thought an atheistic monastery that's just like you but I still can't see you in contemplative mode. You said you all work in the mornings from early, gardening cleaning but what of the afternoons what are they for if not meditation quiet thinking but you were never good at that your enthusiasms always went to extremes and I worry now picturing other saints in the Gallery Anthony or Jerome and just hope you haven't taken up self-flagellation or mortification and I'm not there to tend to appear only when you haven't, for whatever reason, purchased a valid ticket. Fortunately my balletic fellow traveller confirmed that not only was it not operating but still had possession of all his twenty pound note and that the train company were effectively in receipt of excess fare, for which he may sue them. I also showed them my season ticket for work, arguing that although it was for travel in the opposite direction, it did at least prove that I was not by nature a fare dodger.

The upshot, when all had calmed, was that I bought return tickets for myself and my (now) travelling companion, who turned out to be neither ballet dancer nor lawyer, but a professional bore.

He waited for the anxiety to register on my face before

explaining that he was a soil and minerals analyst, working presently in the construction industry in test bores for high-rise foundations, which I found, as I told him, a fascinating coincidence. Even more so, he'd recently completed one in Staines for a projected residential block near the river; too near, in his opinion.

On enquiry, he gave me a detailed description of the whole procedure: setting up the rig, which he liked to supervise in person; drilling down, attaching more and more lengths of tubing as the bit worked down; lifting and numbering the sections; extracting the core and reassembling the sequence to give a diachronic geological snap-shot of the ground beneath one's feet. I must confess I found it all a little too terminologically exact to follow in detail, but the principle intrigues me. It's not unlike my own idea with this project.

19.00 Expanse of green playing field, closely mown cricket square upper right of centre, rusting wire mesh fencing immediate foreground.
Wide-angle: Further expanse of grass, oak trees, to right. To left, window edge, beige window surround giving way to red and blue check upholstery, partial face comprising spike of blond hair, ear, eye (blue), mouth (open), chin (clean shaven) and neck disappearing into yellow polo shirt.

(SAVE/<u>DELETE</u>)

We passed Syon Lane, were approaching Kew Bridge. I mentioned the Water Works tower, leaned across to point it out, feeling some resistance as I did so, a tug on the fabric of my trousers. I felt carefully under my leg, confirming what I suspected. I'd been sitting on a wad of **gum bleeding, that's a sign of scurvy.**

- It's a sign of having your teeth punched out. Who you been narking?

- No one. Narking no one. I'd know wouldn't I?

- Not in your fuckn state. Cut your bleeding ear off you

wouldn't know till you put your hat on.

- Haven't got a hat. Never wear a hat.

- Should in this weather. Kep the sun off.

- They say sunshine's good for you. Gives you vitamin C, like oranges.

- That would stop scurvy.

- So how come sailors got it? Got plenty of sunshine.

- Will you all shut up about fuckn scurvy. Beginning to nark *me*. Reminds me. Still want to know who narked on me to the Bennies.

- Be none of us.

- Neighbour?

- Why?

- Jealous.

- Of me? Why the fuck should anyone be jealous of me?

- Free and easy. Your own man.

- Even when you can't stand up.

- Wouldn't be T would it?

- T? Why?

- For your own good, like. Cut your benefits you'll get less booze.

- T'd never do that. He's straight up.

- Square. T-square. Yeah? No, he's reformed.

- Exactly. Doesna think like us no more.

- If I thought it was T I'd be right fuckn round. Have it out.

- Put it to him straight up.

- Right fuckn round. Soon as the ground stops its fuckn tilt – roofed – literally, as the building, roof and wall, was designed to resemble a military campaign tent, tucked away in a secluded corner of the garden, by the river – a delightful little folly, but almost impossible to spot from the train unless you know it's there.

I would have pointed it out to my fellow traveller but he'd alighted at Chiswick, without, I now realized, making note of my address to refund me his fare, which he'd apparently been anxious to do. It may have been a genuine oversight.

I settled back into my customary aloneness and admired the view. (I've never been able to read in trains; there's an endless cinema through the window.)

The light, richening with the evening, falling on the river beneath Barnes Bridge, its obliquity pointing the rowers in their scull, a heron stationed in the mud. Which gleamed in a stranded inlet mercury-grey, like some Arthurian **mere five K. would lock you into a bond that allows you to unleash the potential of the old Footsie magic, without all the faffle of actually owning shares. The returns are linked to the overall performance of the Footsie One Hundred, averaged out, so your bet is spread, so to speak. Can't go wrong. Five years from now, you'll reap the rewards. You'd naturally like to discuss it with your lady wife? Of course, you must. What's yours is hers, understood ... She's still stuck on Gilts, then? Name's not Prudence? ... No no, understood. Sound reasoning. Pity, that's all ... Not claiming my motives are altogether altruistic, of course - have to earn a crust from the deployment of my expertise - but there's a degree of satisfaction also in pointing out a good opportunity, see someone realize his full potential, financially speaking. But no, point of principle, never advise an investment that your good wife would jib** almost vertical, top section angled down a few degrees, motionless at this time of day, so its silhouette against the skyline matched that of the heron. Not just a visual rhyme but a semantic one, a pun, which I found delightful.

As the train curved round Wandsworth I saw a cluster of them caught by the light, poised as if for take-off, the whole flock. A reminder of the unceasing change, incessant building in the heart of London. Good for the profession, of course, but unsettling for Londoners, I imagine. Neighbourhoods, both residential and working, caught in the flux, bearings constantly revised. An immense and inexplicable sadness descended.

I couldn't shake it off until I joined the familiar bustle of Waterloo. Even then, as I crossed the footbridge to the Shell tower, I glimpsed yet another **jib filling and the spray on his face but it's not, he knows it's not, spray but the bubbles bursting in the mineral water, beading his nose so he tilts his head, his cheek over the glass, allows the bubbles to film over his face, then his ear so the noises of the hostel fade, he's back again entirely in his mind, focusing on the drift, slew, past gone, forgotten for this instant, even - bubbles tickling his eyelids - the wind's spray, sudden bluster driving the acid back into his face as the mail van reversed screeching from the yard** from the platform but the audience was sparse, many at the Proms, so I took a chance and moved further back. No one seemed to mind.

I was unable, for the same reason, to dispose of my spare ticket (I always buy two, in case), so I could spread myself, avoid sitting on the sticky patch on my trousers.

I had assumed the concert was in the Festival Hall, had charged in to find it almost empty, and was directed by the posters to the Queen Elizabeth Hall. I just made it, with time to find, then change, my seat and buy a programme. I switched off my mobile in response to the reminder, and, to be on the safe side, the camera, and settled down at last to relax.

I wasn't sure what to expect. I had booked purely on the programme's theme – A Walk Upon The Beach. It had sounded summery when I booked in rainy March. But the first work - Barber's 'Dover Beach', a setting of Matthew Arnold's poem, for baritone and string quartet – was anything but. Bleak, in fact. The long withdrawing roar of retreating faith, armies clashing by night.

The next, the title work for the concert, was more like it; by a neglected English composer called Forbes Bryson (neglected by me, certainly; I'd never heard of him). A setting of Eliot's 'Love Song Of J. Alfred Prufrock' for tenor, piano quintet and glockenspiel. Rather Expressionist, like early Schönberg, in places, but with a very effective motif on cello and glockenspiel for the crab's ragged scuttling on silent seafloors, later used to undercut the chatter over the teacups; and a haunting ending, the walk upon the beach in flannels (the tenor suddenly and briefly unaccompanied), the mermaids' song in the strings, the sudden drown.

The interval (I didn't go out) was followed by the last work, a short, rarely-heard piece by Harrison Birtwistle.

An early experience of his work had rather put me off him. In my impecunious student days, which for an architect last into early middle age, I'd got a cheap seat for 'The Triumph Of Time' at the Festival Hall. The seats were cheap because they were the unused chorus seats behind the orchestra. Mine was immediately behind the percussion, which play a prominent role in the piece.

But there was no danger of deafness tonight, safely in front of the platform for a work scored only for soprano, three clarinets, piano and marimba.

It was called 'La Plage' and based, surprisingly, I thought, on a short story by Robbe-Grillet, concerning three children walking along a beach in summer, suddenly hearing, above the bird calls and waves, the irregular chime of a distant bell. This provides the whole structure of the piece – the regular patterns of the footsteps, waves and birds, disrupted by the unpredictability of the bell.

Although little-known, the work exemplifies in concentrated form Birtwistles's compositional approach, which I found theoretically enthralling (I spent the whole interval devouring the programme note). It's based on the simple idea of subverted regularity, analogous to the operation of chance and necessity in nature.

To this end, he has adapted a mediaeval technique, of superimposing patterns of different lengths, for example, a rhythmic pattern of six notes, repeated five times, over a melodic pattern of five notes repeated six times. So although beginning and ending together, the differing wave-lengths, as it were, will throw up chance convergences.

But the interaction is subjected to further disruption by

aleatory procedures, the use of random numbers, computer-generated in some cases. Thus, in 'La Plage', subtitled 'Eight Arias of Remembrance', uniform patterns of twelve notes and eight notes, the order of the notes dictated by each being assigned a random number, produce the eight instrumental arias, interleaved by the soprano voicing the children's response to the bell. There are further compositional manoeuvres: rotation of the patterns, alternation between clarinets and piano … I awaited the piece with great interest.

And I enjoyed it.

But I have to confess to getting a little lost early on, whereupon my mind drifted back to the concept of randomness and regularity.

There is, after all, a recognized connection between architecture, music and mathematics. The Greeks equated all three, demonstrated the numerical ratios of harmony and proportion. The whole history of architecture has been premised on that, from the Classical, through the Renaissance application of laws of perspective and harmony, to Le Corbusier and beyond - strict symmetry, irregular symmetry, the Golden Section, the Fibonacci Series - the 'masterly play of masses in light'.

But there has to be an element of randomness, of complexity, to offset sterility – complexity is life. Where does randomness creep in? In the interior, it comes in with the residents, who, despite the best efforts of certain architects, carry chaos, variousness, unpredictability with them. But on the exterior?

Maybe that's why I have always believed architecture to be as much a matter of texture as harmonious mass. Brick, stone, wood – all bring their microcosmic randomness of texture, along, now, with still-living organic elements – plants, vines, grass. It's why the Modernist dream of pure white facades, the Brutalist dream of smooth, unweathering concrete, have failed. Life lies in the quirk.

Silence, then applause, broke my meditation.

I stood up, to find that sitting awkwardly for so long had

induced twinges of sciatica. And I needed a drink.

I limped to the bar, arriving well behind the main crush. I stood to the side, attempting to attract the attention of the barman, listening to the conversations around me, divided mainly among the weather, the music, and the deficiencies of the wine list above the bar, and remembering why it was I now so rarely attend live concerts. One group in particular, who must have booked their seats on the basis of their proximity to the bar, and already enjoying their drinks without moving away from it, were arranging their second, possibly third, while I still waited. The man, in white dinner jacket, was saying 'G and Ts all round again?' One of the women, in silk shawl, fluttered 'No no, I shouldn't. Well, just a teensy one, a **Ginette fast asleep, her bedside light still on. I tiptoed in, turned it off, sure it would wake her. She slept on. I stood in the penumbra of the hallway light watching, seeing her again as a child, lying as now with her arm crooked over her face, as if to shield herself from harm. There was no harm then.**

Will you two ever meet, my love? Will you still be around when she attains that degree of maturity that will allow me to drop the pretence of an idyllic marriage, explain to her that what her mother and I had was most certainly valuable, at times beautiful, but never perfect, could never have been, given the flaws of our nature? When I can finally take off the balance wheels, risk her falling off. Even risk explaining the details of her mother's death?

Say you'll still be here. Please? It's so much to ask. And would you two get on? She looks so like Clair, frighteningly so at times, as Clair looked in her prime numbers might be one example. Their distribution - the occurrence and size of the gaps between them - appear haphazard, theoretically unpredictable.

But some mathematicians doubt not just the randomness of primes and computer-generated random numbers, but randomness in principle, argue that, like fractals in reverse, if the order of magnification, as it were, is increased, there may exist patterns underlying the pseudo-randomness, that are simply beyond our present reasoning. You may perhaps agree with this.

But I still feel that the case for randomness is persuasive, even though there is no agreed definition of it (and if there were it would be either infinitely regressive, or paradoxical - in that having defined its property, that number is no longer random).

My head was beginning to spin, even without the drink, which was at last being poured and passed across to me. I stretched out to take it as someone stepped back at the smash of a falling glass, violently jogging my shoulder.

Whether it was the jog or the penny dropping, I suddenly felt I understood, not just the idea, but the need for randomness, in an almost physical experience, a breath of fresh air in the stuffy bar. I can't express it in mathematical terms, but it's logically simple - that if mathematics proceeds purely by reasoning from defined axiomatic statements, then however complex the results, there can be no surprises, so no creativity; we are merely unpacking the axioms. Everything is ultimately predetermined.

I grasped, at a deeper level, I suppose the aesthetic level, what Birtwistle was doing in 'La Plage', in all his music, perhaps.

I carried what was left of my drink outside onto the terrace and sipped it slowly, looking out over the river. It was slightly warm by then (the wine, that is) but, with the breeze up the Thames, wonderfully refreshing. I felt oddly elated.

I also felt hungry. Apart from the salted almonds in the bar with Richard, I'd had nothing since lunch. I made my way down the steps to the shops and restaurants below the Festival Hall.

I couldn't resist a quick browse in the CD shop first. No sign of the Birtwistle piece on disc, but I did buy The Triumph Of Time. I owe it a proper hearing, controlled, through my headphones. And the Szymanowski Stabat Mater for Richard. A peace offering.

Then I found a noodle bar, slightly less crowded than the other restaurants. I even managed to bag a seat - stool, actually - by the window. I could look out over the river again, at exactly the same view but from a different angle, like twisting the barrel of a kaleidoscope. So the lights from Terry Farrell's Embankment Place danced on the water with the lights of the Embankment, those from the Hungerford Bridge, the Eye behind, but all in a subtly different pattern.

The waitress brought me my plate of noodles with pork dumplings and beans in soy sauce, with a side dish of brown rice. She was young, looked Chinese herself, and I wondered if she were happy, and how different her life might be, have been, had she or her family stayed in China. I thought of her being on opposite production ends of the rice I was eating – serving it up in overlit cosmopolitan London, when she could so easily be growing it, wading at dawn through lonely **paddy with me darling. You knew about Rupert all along. I made no secret of him. And no, it wasn't for comparison, or to keep you on your toes. That's a horrid thing to say. Look, I didn't know he was coming, didn't even know he was in the country, I've only this minute had his text. No it most certainly was not arranged, and if you seriously think I get off on having grown men resort to fisticuffs over me you're even** *madder or crimson lake for the central gash cheating really but it's watercolour decompose along with the rest can't be arsing around plant-hunting anymore get it finished exorcism started take the first snap today not flash natural daylight sun's already well on its verge* over the eaves where they nest, but there are fewer and fewer such old buildings in London, and they don't seem to take to flat-roof overhangs and service-cranes, so my guess is that the sight of swifts in London and along the Thames corridor will become increasingly rare, one day a thing of the past. To have seen them tonight seems a benediction of sorts. Good omen, too, so high up at dusk. A sign the good weather's going to last, until tomorrow at least.

Although according to the long-range forecast, the good weather may outlast the swifts - they'll be gone by next month.

22.00 Expanse of paving immediate foreground, flanked by eight-stranded cable fencing, tubular steel handrails. To left, angled pylon, steel rods radiating from top of pylon (out of frame) to below paving. To right, similar rods, further pylon, seen complete with pulley, rods to walkway, rods at more acute angle, to pontoon.

Wide-angle: to left, Westminster skyline, floodlit, through grid of railway bridge; to right, Embankment Place (part-obscured), church spire, foliage, illuminated boats.

(<u>SAVE</u>/DELETE)

After my usual gaze downriver from Hungerford Bridge for a last glimpse of St. Paul's in the dying light, I walked slowly back to Waterloo. The sciatica had eased but my ankle was throbbing.

I had time to spare, even so – my train was in, but not due to depart for another ten minutes. I walked halfway down the train, equivalent to where the exit would be at my station, entered the empty carriage. I glanced up as I did so, to the iron pillars and girders of the roof. A pigeon was fluttering back and forth, its efforts to perch frustrated by the spikes and netting.

I thought again of the swifts searching for nest space. It struck me forcibly that we, humans in general but architects in particular, think in terms of purely human habitation in our buildings, forget the creatures that share our habitat. It's easy to forget we are part of a web, ramifying beyond us, that we're interdependent on what we can't see.

A simple enough matter to leave chinks in the gables, a recessed brick. But it's not just birds that are hard-pressed to survive. Bees, butterflies … Grassed roofs are gaining recognition for their cooling effect, on high-rise especially. Why not a grass-and-clover mix, or wild meadow flowers? The acreage would soon mount up in urban areas.

Our whole architectural approach, in fact, will have to change, radically maybe, in the not-distant future. Climatic developments will force us to rethink many standard practices. Stronger winds are predicted, a widening of the tornado belts. So stress levels may have to be recalibrated, especially for cantilevers. In time, the whole cantilever principle may have to be abandoned, along with ultra-high rise, the skyscraper mentality.

Higher temperatures all round, but heat islands in particular - urban centres averaging up to 10° higher than the surrounding mean – will dictate new designs. Not just natural ventilation and cooling systems, but structure and materials rethought. The abandonment of curtain wall and cladding in favour of solid, massive construction, for example. Which raises the further issues of sustainability and recyclability. Thick-poured concrete would give the thermal advantages of solidity, but could be re-used only as hardcore. Even my beloved bricks, though salvageable to a degree, may not be the answer.

But I've noticed lately a renewed interest in natural stone. Mostly in the form of light cladding, which of course uses less stone, but causes more wastage, and gives more aesthetic than thermal benefits. I have seen in the trade press, though, examples of larger, whole-stone construction, which initially appears to use more resources, but in the long term, doesn't. If the stones are load-bearing, other materials are saved; and after demolition, the larger the stones, the more re-usable, unlike tailor-made cladding panels. The Peake, Short brewery project in Malta is one that impressed me. Malta is hotter than London, but in time, London will be as hot (and Malta hotter).

Or Ian Ritchie's use of gabion walls, first in France, later in London. Gabions are a good example of old methods brought up to date: wire mesh (originally wicker) cages filled with stone rubble, which can be of any size, allowing the use of discarded stone, with the further advantage in that they can be loosely packed to allow light and air to filter through, or densely packed against water seepage, or earthed and seeded, to enhance the cooling.

But even solid, dressed-stone walls can be made porous to light and breeze. One project I read of, I think in Japan, used regular 12inch cut slabs laid with regular gaps, like slits, some glazed, some open, so from inside, against the light, the wall resembled chain-**mail? Ah, yes. No. *Post*. The President is perhaps thinking of The Last Post. But that is played on the bugle, for the lowering of the flag. This is a medley, on the bagpipes, for one's enjoyment. And to make the President feel at home. The bagpipes, one understands, originated in the Islamic lands?**

My husband and I fondly remember the Britannia being serenaded off the Bosphorus by a veritable brigade of bagpipers in their skirted uniform. My husband was reminded of the Dagenham Girl Pipers. Of course, bagpipes have a different name in Turkey, and a different name again, one assumes, in Turkmenistan? You don't? Well, never mind. But if the President really is enjoying this, he must visit us again, come to Balmoral, enjoy a full military tattoo over one side of his shaven head and face, his neck, and down one arm. I thought of Queequeg in Moby Dick. He turned out to be equally harmless. In fact, it wasn't his appearance that caused people in the carriage to shrink at his approach, but his speech, a long, apparently rehearsed or previously-used spiel about being let down over his supply of Big Issues, that he'd been promised them faithfully by the morning, no problem with the printing, no problem there, but he still needed tonight's takings to secure a bed at the hostel, so any donations or advance sales would be gratefully received. Despite, or maybe because of, the glibness of the spiel, he had a sheepish air as he moved down the carriage, ignored.

I let him pass, followed him out the door, slipped him a tenner. He was happy to accept, no scruples over 'street aid' with him. It's possible the whole thing was a fraud, but I'd rather not risk its being genuine. I was grateful for being on the way home, to a bed, with clean(ish) sheets, and a nightcap. He, I suspect, would have only the latter.

The atmosphere had thickened perceptibly as I resumed my seat. Even the mobile phone conversations seemed subdued. But as the train got underway it all returned to normal. I took out my notebook and Pelikan and began to sketch, inspired by my earlier thoughts on stone.

I've always liked to draw castles in the air – signature buildings that I know will never be built; indeed, that's the point of them. You, I'm sure, understand the urge for constant creativity; adding to the store of hypothetical realities. It's also good discipline in converting ideas into design, testing feasibility. And who knows, someday a landmark commission could come my way.

So I set myself to envisaging the problems and possibilities of solid-stone construction. The immediate problem is material, which is to say, assuming you're not building adjacent to a quarry, transport. I solved that by choosing a riverside site (as this is hypothetical, I'm allowed to cheat), allowing transport by barge, as in the past.

So, I specified a site on the south bank of the Thames, though not necessarily in London; it could as well be in Staines. This would mean its northern aspect would front the river. The site then raises the problem of flooding. I could overcome that by the use of gabions for the first storey, dense-packed for the first course, loose-packed the second; could even turn it to advantage by using bastions for the first course: gabions with membrane lining on the inner walls, which could act as filters of floodwater and rainwater, to be stored as greywater in basement reservoirs.

The building itself I conceived of first as a ziggurat, then to add a challenge, as ziggurat/reverse ziggurat, the south and east aspects stepped back, in shallow terraces, the north and west aspects correspondingly stepped out, not cantilevered but corbelled, with gaps or venting under each course, to catch and divert the prevailing breeze.

I wanted textural interest too. A gradation of texture, from the roughness of the gabions, through rubble walling, then squared cleft-cut stone, to polished stone for the upper storeys, the rubble and square-cut storeys punched through with full-height windows, internally glazed to increase the sciagraphic effect; the polished levels fretted with small, square windows and horizontal slits.

The roof a shallow south-facing monopitch, recessed to appear flat from ground level, with solar panels and rainwater filters. Finally, the terraces to be planted with alternating upright columnar cypresses and trailing vines, the north- (river-)facing gabions to be earthed and seeded with a wildflower mixture.

All of this would of course have to be assessed technically, but the concept intrigued me, so much so that I nearly passed my stop. I hadn't heard the announcement, and if someone hadn't jogged me as the train jerked, I wouldn't have seen the platform sign either. I just managed to **rally him over his girth but he misses the banter and even Kenny whose jokes sometimes cut had signed the card though probably it was him who'd done the drawing of the whale spouting beside the printed text May Your New Course In Life Lead To Treasure with a cartoon desert island but it was Bas who'd said, Had a whip-round, Col, got you this, you won't be able to sleep in the buff now, maid'll mistake you for Moby Dick, and Jackson who'd said, Yeah, wear this and be mistaken for the island instead, and when he'd opened the nightshirt it was still in its wrapper but they must have taken it out, resealed it, because they'd added four more Xs to the label, and used indelible ink, a laundry marker maybe, because they still haven't washed out and he's glad of that, glad to be reminded of them all as he pulls the cream Sea Island cotton over his damp hair (the bath had been too small - he'll mark it 3 - he'd used the shower), and he suddenly, piercingly, wishes to be back, even as the butt, the huge butt, of their humour, and as he lowers himself onto the bed, stretches, bounces, settles, he feels himself - returning their joke - a *maroon? This is Samarkand Plum with Wild Honey highlights, I'll have you know. And to be blunt, aren't***

you a teensy bit pot-calling-the-kettle-black? I don't remember
your hair being quite so swarthy before. Actually I liked you
grey. It's distinguished. Distinguishes you from younger men.
No, I'm teasing, darling. No, I don't want a younger man.
Really, Rupert, I'm just so so pleased you're back. Sugar daddy?
Certainly not. Who says I call you Mr. Tate? Bitch. And if I
did, I was only referring to your mooching round the galleries
for hours. Yes I know it's your stock in trade, though you've
never exactly explained what your trade is. No, I don't want to
come with you. Crippled after an hour. And I refuse to wear
pumps, even for you. Feel like one of those ghastly tourists, in
Cavalli and trainers. Apparently, during the war, the National
salted away all their paintings in a Welsh cave, just had one
on display each day. Much more civilized. But there are still
the crowds. Besides, I'm not silly enough to think it's my mind
you're after, improved or unimproved. But what you men don't
understand, darling - and I especially mean succesful men - is
that we have a more limited shelf-life than you. You have to
capitalize your assets, isn't that what you keep telling me, every
business trip? I don't want to look back on my life and see long
wastes of frump. But honestly, darling, it doesn't mean I'm not
yours, heart and soul. Jago and Nigel and Simon - oh, didn't
you? - they're just fun. But it wouldn't be fun if I didn't have
you to, well, be there. Now this is getting morbid. So. Stop
sulking. I'll slip on this lovely Phillip Lim and we'll go out on
the lash the shore, wave after breaking wave and even the
most obdurate granite succumbs grain by grain to the
neutral attrition, even the Rock worn smooth has
surrendered edges. Yet what happens, I have to ask, to the
particled rock? I begin to recognize, in my fumbling way,
an eternal process at work. For that surrendered rock exists
still as rock, albeit in suspension, settling into patient
sediment, awaiting that metamorphic pressure. And in all
this do I glimpse, do I dare catch at a glimpse, of hope or
at the least of an unconstraining? Of a however distant

resolving of suspension, into a sedimentary critical mass? A way forward? And am I to grasp that the suspension's resolving is by - but mine or Thine? - forgiveness lash the tiller and sink himself into his bunk, listening to wave after wave breaking on the hull, commit himself to swell and current and tidal pull, trust himself to the oceanic flow, slide, toward childish hope in a childhood insinuation, of a soft white eraser, a magic slate, forgiveness. He will-dreams himself, in his narrow bunk, to a distant harbour, warp secured, *marled field beyond the quarry, to be cropped once more, then similarly gouged for gravel. Who knows what, or who, will be unearthed, a sleep of how many generations disturbed? For they would have settled widely, no constraining river or tarmacked airport to pen them to the quarry site alone. Hordes, there may be, unoblivious. The whole field a grave, 'marl'd with bleaching bones'. Where does that come from? Coleridge, he thinks, tries to recall exactly, in conscious distraction, but the distraction's not strong enough, he turns himself instead to his wife in an ecstasy of thanks, for her whiteness is the whiteness of flesh, not bone, and he grasps out, and she, grown unused to spontaneity,* Wakes Weeks when, he thought, the town would be quiet, deserted maybe, with the factories closed, everyone on holiday. He'd taken the bus, crossed counties, to add to the adventure, to look round without moythering crowds, see for himself, something to boast about to himself. But he'd got off the bus at its turning yard, not known where to head for, there were no proper signs, only road names, he'd wandered around, past the Town Hall that appeared to be empty, round some corners, into a road that wasn't empty at all, people everywhere, criss-crossing the road reckless of traffic. He'd thought from the busyness it must lead to the town centre so he'd started down it, but it seemed all pubs, one after another, or take-out food shops, and the paving was clarted with sick and the rowdiness wasn't like in the village pub, even after dipping's over, so he'd gone back, retraced his route, right back to the bus yard, got on the next one home. But on the bus, as it went uphill and turned a corner, he'd glimpsed a grand gold dome, glowing against the hills and peaks. He'd twisted in his seat as the bus turned again but he didn't see it anymore. He's remembered it ever since, though, something he'd taken home with him. Still, he'd been pleased to get home. He'd sat on the stile on Lower Ridge, for his family weren't expecting him home till night, he didn't want to admit his funk, so he sat and thought of the golden dome, and the green fields and smell of the sheep, then walked to the village, bought some cheese baps. And Velta whispers, *ja, razumem,* and cuts him more pizza, and says, as he eats, So, I think you had great - *kako se re ce?* - bravery, no, in following to London, and he shrugs and smiles and says, You know I'd follow you anywhere, and he feels he's being prompted to ask Velta the inevitable but wants to backtrack for the umpteenth time, chews the pizza crust slowly, but then there's the **boom** of a plane beyond the reservoir, and he blurts, Do they have sheep in Slovenia? Would they need shepherds? And she says, Sheep, farms, of course. But she says many are giving up now, going for cutting trees, making cars, many now she thinks will follow like her to France, Ukay. In her grandparents' region already some farms were for sale. He says, Some? How many? She counts on her fingers, holds up five, says, *Pet, Marigold. It's a livelihood for them, not a hobby. Yes, I did, and you can. I just think you ought to, well, prepare yourself, emotionally, first. Tell you what we'll do. We'll have pork chops for tomorrow's supper, and if you feel no qualms after that, we'll give the go-ahead to your little chappie on the sty. No. Yes, of course I enjoyed the sea bass. No, you're deliberately missing the point. Well, I don't know. However you like. How does one normally serve them? Grilled, with a sprinkling of rosemary, and a decent Riesling, I* *suppose.* **All right, then. Liver and bacon, bacon and egg, pork scratchings and a tin of bloody** Fosters a misleading image, I suppose. People always expect architects to live in some all-glass thing they've designed themselves. But apart from not having the time to design and build for myself when struggling to establish the practice – cobblers go unshod – I loved this house, still do: a sturdy late-Victorian red and buff brick semi-detached, with a beautiful on-edge basketweave gable and (now renovated) sash windows. I also resisted any pressure to gut it and reconfigure the interior. In fact, apart from installing a deep-bore ground pump, and converting the kitchen to a studio with a drop-in modular galley in the pantry (I don't cook), and the inevitable replastering, I've kept it as I bought it, right down to the Fifties formica cupboards. I don't see them ironically; I like the palimpsest of changing tastes, of sequential lives predating mine. To me, it's home.

23.00

I arrived home a little before eleven, switched off my phone, disconnected the spycam from my spectacles, put some coffee on to brew while I had a shower.

I took out the concert programme to reread in bed, remembered the Szymanowski CD in the other pocket. I considered wrapping it, but I felt that would be overdoing it, underlining the apology. I'll give it to Richard just as it is in the shrink wrap. I peeled off the price tag and put it into my briefcase.

As I did do I was confronted by the buff envelope of my X-rays. I slit it open. It contained, with the plates, a sealed envelope addressed to my G.P. and a note advising me to hand the X-rays in to my surgery immediately, and make an appointment to see my doctor within a week. That too I returned to my briefcase for action in the morning.

But today, while it still is today, I wish to finish this project.

I downloaded the hourly snaps, began the transcription.

And now, approaching midnight, zero-hour (time distorts; it may be later), it is finished. Sign off the project. Leave it to find its niche in posterity. You approve, I hope. Mundane factness; how things happened to be. Our only possible offering.

Yet already, the moment it is finished, I have the gravest misgivings. Looking back over my day, my life, its texture of relationships, it all seems suddenly so tenuous, so touch-and-go, so mockingly fragile.

The unexamined life is not worth living (Plato? Aristotle?), perhaps. And the unrecorded life is wasted. But the examined life may no longer be livable.

One feels so exposed, so vulnerable. Lonely, in a word.

I read recently of an experimental site being built in the Alps, a long subterranean tunnel, like an expanded Circle Line. When it's finished in five years' time, electrons will be split off, whipped up to near the speed of light, allowed to collide; just to see what happens. Pulsing round the circuit, prey to randomness. You understand. You may sympathize, even, with that lone electron. Maybe it all makes sense at a higher level, builds into some larger pattern.

I've changed my mind about the Szymanowski; I will gift-wrap it. It may be, who knows, a farewell present.
I had some wrapping paper left from Linda's last birthday. I don't suppose Richard will recognize it.

Yes, about enough left. The CD has slipped down the compartment of my briefcase, among the flooring estimates, veneer samples, catalogues and subscription reminders, all the architectural bric-à-brac I keep meaning to clear out.

Maybe I should scan them into the project, or better, attach them physically in some way, with my bus and concert tickets, Big Issue copy, bar receipts … Material actuality has a solidity beyond its weight. Whether the actuality of the paper will survive as long as the file may be doubtful.

There again, it may well outlive it. There are now serious questions raised about the life span of digital texts. All these books, manuscripts, archives committed to disc may be mouldering far slower than the shiny shellac, the virtual library. Some archivists, I believe, have grave misgivings.

What *will* survive of us? (Love, said Larkin, but I'm not sure he believed it.) What of us will trickle through the filters of time into posterity? And will that posterity be a virtual universe? As possibly ephemeral as the digital archive?

In my moments of pessimism, which are becoming more frequent (isn't pessimism supposed to be the ultimate blasphemy?) I find myself foundering in the present. I have nightmares involving Piranesian buildings, all of them deserted.

Right now, alone in the light of my desk-lamp, I can picture quite clearly the building I sketched on the train, complete, weathered, the plantings matured; eerily empty.

Not 'bare ruin'd choirs'; still entirely intact, each joint, joist and detail evidencing the **toil of his limbs but she had resisted, assuming he'd mistaken the day, unaware of the urgency beyond the physical, leaving him trying to content himself with just holding her hand, pulling her arm over as she lies on her side, turned away, burrowing back into sleep. Squeezing it harder but still unable to drag her back, he lies stiffened beside her, thinking, afraid, of the pit, of the sown field, beyond, sulphur yellow in the sun, of rape-*wine he'd got going from the skins of the Seyval Blanc, decides to check on it, seeing a plan of campaign. He puts down his nightcap - Damson, Special Reserve - goes through to the scullery, finds the labelled demijohn. Maybe a little premature for its last racking but he feels reckless, faint heart never won... draws off a good three* gills venting as it lies in the grass, thrashing finished with, resigned now, like a sheep in the shearsman's** hold. He watches as the life ticks out. Scales gleam silver in the sickly moonlight, a few of them scuffed off onto his sleeve, his trouser leg, as he'd fumbled the disgorger, now glint like mercury drops at his every movement. He soaks a rag, wraps it round it, to keep it fresh and cover its eyes, lays it in a shadowed hollow. He checks the cast with his fingertips, washes the hook, rebaits. He's enough for breakfast but he's too excited, he knows, for sleep. Whatever else he catches he'll return to the water. He casts underarm, upstream, allowing himself to be mesmerised by the flourescent quill, but listens, grins, as a plane, the last of the night, lifts behind him, turns to watch its lights winking through the *paling in the moonlight as I switched off her bedside light, took the book from the duvet. She looked so self-assured, yet so vulnerable, and (Oh God, let it all come right) I decided to do as you said, and despite my lectures on extravagance, buy her that new tennis* racket of a won-over audience *rooting peaceably, comfortingly, on the* lawn skirt and blouse, there, at the back of the window, see it darling? in lavender. That would be really divine, and economical, because I've already got that mauve Hermès scarf prised, penetrated, the bastions silted, underfloor reservoirs stagnant, the water *stale gushing between its legs and its eyes rolling like the horse in that painting by Picasso and just before I woke I just knew its hoof was viced in a* gin and tonic from the minibar, carries it back to bed but knowing it will take several more to send him to sleep, and tries to remember the name, Greek? Latin? 'bread' in it, of the character who offered lodgings to travellers, then made them fit the dimensions of the bed, short men stretched, tall men *tailed all the way home from the... alright, I'm sorry, didn't mean to wake you, but the bastards are making sure I don't do a fucking* bunk... *course I am. They're so fucking determined I face this* rap against the lightless windows and the roots and tendrils pry.

And now that I have to confront the vision, I must accept the logical extension to the adjacent buildings, one after the other, all along the riverfront like darkened theatres while below them the sweet Thames runs softly. Accept too the extension in time, for who is there, in the dream-logic, to restore and re-inhabit? The Thamesmeads flood, buildings become barrows. Our clients and their offspring turned off the estate with seraphs posted round the *fence? Doesn't sound like you, Rupert. Flashing the épées seems far too energetic for you.   Not that sort? Well, I can hardly see you knocking posts in, that's even more preposterous, and I can't think... oh, God. OH   MY   GOD. All the money you spend on me comes from...? Well, business. You never said what. Business is just business to me. You were always pretty cagey, so... What do you mean, no worse than me? Just who the hell are you calling a* tart, almost vinegary. Just the stuff. Sort the men from the boys. Or codgers. Print a flowery label, take the bottle down to the club on a night when Valerie's there, watch her watch their faces as they sip, while he effortlessly downs his glassfull, casually mentions the proof. Should recoup a little kudos. He fetches a newly sterilized bottle, an empty demijohn, carries on racking my brains trying to remember the exact quotation. You of course would know it.

But it occurs to me, sharply, that if the vision were true, if indeed posterity is no longer to be relied on, entertained, is a thing of the past, my project carries an even greater poignancy.

For this – my day, my life, the lives of those I touch – has happened; out of all the possible synaptic contacts, this is what my memory records. This is history, *my*story.

I came across a quotation somewhere to the effect that 'not even God can abolish historical fact.' Only You can confirm the truth of that.

But I can only see from my own perspective. And the immediate problem, which for me is how to go on living the examined life. I am only beginning to see the implications.

To accept contingency, randomness, as the ground of our freedom? I've decided already to tear up the X-rays. I've no wish to know. It's not foolhardiness. Everything now is called into question.

Further, to accept, embrace, our loneliness, as the price we pay, each of us, for our uniqueness? For if we are each unique, we are inescapably lonely.

And as a corollary, to accept, to be both chastened and comforted by the fact, that as our solitary paths cross and collide, we are liable to leave only hurt, damage in our ***wake ... a wake ...lapping ...awake ...wake ...***

What's to be salvaged from all this? I'm trying to find some illuminating, over-arching metaphor in it all. Without success. Life is its own metaphor. I remember now another quotation I once copied down, though I can't remember its source:

"The world is both empirical and contingent; but only from beyond, from without, the grid. From within, it cannot be questioned. And therein lies our place; there we find our role."

... lapping... awake... wake...

Resolve